Reciprocity

Reciprocity

Lori G. Moses

Writer's Showcase
presented by *Writer's Digest*
New York San Jose Lincoln Shanghai

Reciprocity

All Rights Reserved © 2000 by Lori G. Moses

No part of this book may be reproduced or transmitted in any form or by any means, graphic, electronic, or mechanical, including photocopying, recording, taping, or by any information storage retrieval system, without the permission in writing from the publisher.

Writer's Showcase
presented by *Writer's Digest*
an imprint of iUniverse.com, Inc.

For information address:
iUniverse.com, Inc.
620 North 48th Street, Suite 201
Lincoln, NE 68504-3467
www.iuniverse.com

ISBN: 0-595-12060-1

Printed in the United States of America

*To my father
who instilled in me a love for words
and to my mother
who always encouraged me to use them*

Acknowledgments

This book would not have been written without the unending support of my good friends. To Pamela Signorella, for nurturing words and humor; to Rindi Tarlow, for editing with respect for my many anxieties; to Gail Michele for countless consultations; to Helen Chisholm and Deirdre Johnson, for crucial spiritual interpretation and larger perspectives.

A special thanks to Dorothy Thompson, for karmic parallels and page-by-page critique; and to my anonymous friend, who was there from the inception—I am grateful for the opportunity to know you.

And finally, to all those women in Boston, Cambridge, Springfield and Long Island, who, from 1981 to the present, have courageously shared their pain, with the hope of healing their remaining scars and moving on. Your stories have not been forgotten.

Chapter 1

Pamela Windsor arrived twenty minutes early for her counseling appointment. She appeared nervous at the registration desk, and was given the usual demographic paperwork for new patients to complete. She sat down in a chair in the Access Health Center's waiting room, and in a moment, she was standing again, to straighten her skirt. With the clipboard and paperwork in one hand, she positioned her skirt with the other, and this time, seemed to have found a comfortable position to begin.

Pamela appeared troubled, and in fact, had difficulty with the simplest questions. I'm not sure of who I am, she thought, as she wrote her name in the spaces provided. Windsor is not my real last name, she thought, and promised herself she would attempt to tell her counselor this evening about her adoption. Being adopted had not bothered her until her nineteenth birthday. In fact, she reminisced, my adoptive father has been so kind, so good to me, I should be grateful. It was on her nineteenth birthday that Pamela's first boyfriend, Brian Carlson, told her he wanted to end their relationship. Pamela cried until her eyes hurt, and since then, crying had become a daily chore for her, like making her bed and cleaning the kitchen after dinner. Without Brian, she felt so lost and alone. Pamela had few girlfriends, and they mostly got together to party, not to talk. So she had plenty of time to think about rejection. First, by her birth mother, then by her adoptive mother, and finally, by Brian. She had been so conscious of her hurts that she wondered now, how will I trust a counselor?

This thought brought Pamela back to her present assignment, and she continued quickly with her address and telephone number, as well as the pertinent information about her employment and insurance. Thank goodness, she thought, I do have a good job. Pamela was an Administrative Assistant for several engineers in a large electronics firm in Springfield, Massachusetts. She liked her boss and it was Mr. Hansen who had noticed the recent change in her work performance, calling her into his office to ask if there was anything wrong. Pamela had been mortified to have started crying in front of him, but Mr. Hansen was soft-spoken and patient, and suggested the idea of talking to a professional when Pamela could not explain the cause of her lack of concentration and pain. He had given her the telephone number for Access Health Center, which she later discovered was only a few blocks from work, and she had made an appointment for Monday, January 11th.

The date had arrived quickly. Pamela had felt oddly nervous throughout the weekend before. What will I talk about? She wondered. What will the counselor think of me? How will it help just to talk about my problems? I don't want anyone to know I'm here, Pamela asserted, as she stood to hand the secretary her completed paperwork.

It was comforting to see her counselor reviewing it now. She was glad that the counselor was a young woman, and Pamela was soon being led to a small room with no window. Plants and paintings hung haphazardly, and the couch she sat on was soft, beige and inviting. When the counselor's first words to her had to do with confidentiality, Pamela felt assured that her secrets would be kept. Pamela wanted to trust this woman; she seemed gentle and confident. To her surprise, Pamela became tearful again upon hearing "What brings you here today?" She tried to relax and tell her story.

"I really loved my boyfriend Brian," Pamela explained. "He broke up with me last month, on my birthday, and I've been crying like this ever since. He meant everything to me. I tried to please him; I really tried. I don't know what happened."

"Why did he say he wanted to stop seeing you?"

"He didn't really. I think he must be interested in someone else. Actually, I've passed his house a few times and there's been an extra car in the driveway. I guess I just wasn't good enough for him."

"What makes you say that?"

"Well, I never felt like I was being the way he wanted me to be. I tried to change for him and be what he wanted, but I never was really sure what it was I was doing wrong."

"That sounds very confusing."

"I guess."

"Tell me about you."

"What do you mean?"

"I'd like to know something about your feelings about yourself."

"I HATE MYSELF!"

"Ohhh?"

"I'm sorry. I sound like I'm complaining. But my life never feels like it's going right. It must be my fault. I have no boyfriend, my mother hates me, I have no real friends…I'm sorry I'm crying."

"That's what the tissues are for. No need to apologize."

Pamela reached for two tissues, wiped her eyes, and continued. "He used to get mad at me. I annoyed him. I was always asking him how I looked, what he wanted to do, if he was mad at me. I was always insecure around him. I loved him so much and just wanted to please him."

"What did you love about him?"

Pamela was taken aback. She thought for a while before she answered. "He was good-looking. He played football in high school and he worked out. He had a great red Corvette, an old one that his grandfather gave him. He took great care of that car. Sometimes he took me out to the movies, or to dinner, and I felt so special having him around.

He always wanted…" Pamela trailed off. *I don't know if I should tell her this,* she thought to herself.

"Did you want to finish that sentence?"

"Well, he always wanted to have sex. I'm sorry, I shouldn't have said that, but it was the one way he seemed to be able to show me he cared. He would be affectionate afterward for a little while, and my nervousness would go away."

"Your nervousness?"

"I'm nervous a lot. My father says I care too much about what other people think. He says I'm a good person and I shouldn't worry so much. But…I can't help it. Anyway, I don't agree."

"You don't agree with what?"

"I don't think I'm a good person. Brian said I was an idiot. I think he blamed me…" Pamela stopped short. *I don't know if I can talk about this,* she thought. *Maybe I made a big mistake in coming here.* The counselor interrupted her train of thought.

"Brian blamed you?"

Okay, she's gonna hate me too, but I really need to tell someone. "I got pregnant." Pamela's tears began to flow so hard and her mouth felt so contorted that she was afraid to speak. Slowly, she volunteered, "I can't talk about what happened. My mother would've thrown me out on the street if I had a baby. I don't make enough money to be on my own, and Brian, well, he thought I should have been taking birth control pills. He was so mad when I told him that I thought he was gonna hit me."

"Had he hit you before?"

"Yes, but I deserved it."

"No, you didn't."

Pamela reached for some tissues. She was creating a pile of used tissues in the small garbage pail near her right leg. She stared at the pile, and her eyes were so filled with tears that the tissues became one blur, like a fluffy blur of cotton candy. *Cotton candy,* Pamela thought. *Brian* had bought her cotton candy years ago, at the Big E, an event held right in her hometown of West Springfield. They had had a wonderful day. The Big E was better than a carnival, but that was before all the trouble started. The pregnancy, the clinic visit, borrowing money from her father, lying about where she was going. Pamela knew she was a bad person. "I can't talk about this right now", Pamela whispered to the counselor.

Rachel Abbott-Moss astutely changed the subject, and began asking some simple questions about Pamela's home life, her parents and brother. She asked Pamela if it would be all right to take some notes on her intake form, and Pamela nodded. Pamela was thankful to be talking about other things, and her tears began to subside for the time being.

The session progressed for Rachel Abbott-Moss, the social worker assigned to complete the intake for Pamela Windsor. Pamela provoked images in Rachel's mind of a starving baby bird. She was petite, well-dressed, with blonde hair cut in layers and bright blue eyes, although her eyes were swollen and red from the tears she had shed. This young woman has some secrets, Rachel thought. She seems so naïve and innocent. Rachel vowed to help Pamela ascertain how she herself contributed to her feelings of low self-esteem. Rachel was already hypothesizing that this young woman in her office had been criticized or ridiculed unjustly, and Rachel knew that this could manifest itself in Pamela's need to apologize frequently.

Rachel was a graduate of a prestigious School of Social Work in Western Massachusetts. She had valued her education, and found she was often able to engage clients in conversation which would enhance their understanding of themselves. Rachel enjoyed her work immensely. She remained awed at the complexities of human nature, as well as her clients' abilities to face their own demons with honesty and integrity. Pamela seemed so childlike, Rachel mused. She resolved to move slowly and cautiously with her, allowing Pamela to take control of the information she shared. And Rachel would attempt to demystify the counseling process for Pamela, by making suggestions of books to read as well as by educating her about grief and loss. Before the end of this first session with Pamela, Rachel demonstrated that the theme of her discussion had been about loss. Rachel discussed Elisabeth Kubler-Ross's stages of grief, and spoke for a short while about what to expect in the coming weeks. Rachel noticed Pamela's shoulders slowly drop from the place they had inhabited around her neck, to a more relaxed pose at her sides.

Pamela felt much better, relieved almost, after talking to her new counselor. And it was nice to get some feedback from her, too. Before she could stop herself, Pamela asked, "You mean I'm normal?"

Rachel smiled warmly. "Of course you're normal."

The end of Pamela's first session had arrived so quickly that she was shocked to hear herself say, "Can I come again to see you this week? I don't think I can wait until Monday."

Rachel reached for her appointment book and scheduled Pamela for her second appointment on Thursday, January 14th, after Pamela finished work. Pamela left the room with Rachel, who introduced her to Hilary, the secretary at the reception desk. Rachel smiled and retreated back to her office, leaving Pamela to collect her thoughts and pay for her session. She signed her name to her check with an unsteady hand.

Why am I feeling different? Pamela asked herself. Rachel seemed to have a calming influence on me, she thought. But there's something else, something important, Pamela pondered as she walked to her car, an old Hyundai Excel that Brian used to make fun of. Pamela started the car, and headed home to her parents' house, a small Cape Cod on a cul-de-sac in West Springfield. As she began the short drive north on Route 91, the thought came to her. That something important. It was hope.

Chapter 2

Pamela pulled into her driveway carefully, leaving room for the taxi that would be arriving shortly to transport her mother to dialysis. Her mother received hemodialysis three times per week at an outpatient facility in West Springfield, and arrived home after Pamela was in bed on Mondays, Wednesdays and Fridays. When her mother had first started dialysis, Pamela had gone with her and observed her treatments, keeping her mother company and worrying about her health. Pamela was told when she was very young that her mother had polycystic kidney disease, and that eventually, her kidneys might fail. In fact, this was the main reason her mother was frightened about having her own children, and chose to adopt Pamela. Her mother was often too weak to drive after treatments, and her father often worked late in his law office, so he paid a taxi company to transport her the few miles to Pioneer Valley Renal Center on Ashland Street.

How many times had her father sat her down throughout the past few years to explain to Pamela that her mother was not really mad at her, but was angry about her illness? Countless times. It seemed to Pamela that her mother looked for things to be angry about. Pamela had grown more and more responsible about household chores since her mother's dialysis began. Her mother was often too fatigued to vacuum or carry groceries. So Pamela would do the family's grocery shopping and clean the house as best she could, but it was never good enough for her mother. Pamela reasoned that her mother was angry that she was still a relatively young woman, and it was hard for her to cope with the need for life-sustaining treatment, as well as her limitations. But Pamela's mother had always been critical of her, even before the dialysis began. And sometimes, Pamela's frustration got the better of her, and she would fight with her mother until they both would cry, turning their backs on each other so as not to show their vulnerabilities, and ignore each other for the next few hours.

Her father often returned to a silent home after one of these arguments. Pamela admired her father. He was intelligent, kind and generous. She hated to make his life more stressful, and so she would sit patiently as he convinced her to be the one to apologize to her mother. She would eventually do so, but it was never long before another argument would begin.

Pamela's brother was useless, she thought. He was three years younger and had been conceived by her parents. In Pamela's mind, the fact that he was not adopted contributed to his status as prince in the family. He never lifted a finger to help. Pamela was feeling sorry for herself again, she noticed. She said hello to her mother, explained that she had been out with friends after work, and began straightening up the kitchen. Her parents and brother had already eaten. After her chores were complete, feigning exhaustion, Pamela retired to her room early to read.

Another lie, she thought. Pamela was plagued about her need to lie to her parents. She was unable to tell anyone about Rachel Abbott-Moss, or the events leading up to her decision to see her. She had said she was out with friends. Would she be able to lie every week, maybe twice a week, about where she was going? I'm tired of thinking about things, Pamela thought, and she changed into her nightgown, washed up, and picked up the romance novel that lay on her nightstand. After a few short chapters, though, Pamela's mind drifted and she took comfort in sleep.

* *

The dream began routinely enough. Pamela was traveling to work in her Hyundai Excel, and arrived at the street where Brian lived. As she drove past the split-level homes, a heavy rain began to fall, heavy enough to use the windshield wipers' highest speed. Her sight was obscured by the downpour and Pamela thought she saw a squirrel crossing the road. Pamela turned the steering wheel sharply to avoid hitting the squirrel, and pulled over to the side of the road to calm herself. Her knees felt weak, as she loved all animals, and dreaded being responsible for killing any living creature. When she looked to her left to examine the situation, the dream turned quickly into a nightmare.

There was no squirrel in the road, but an infant, crying and drenched from the rain. Pamela raced to leave her car and lifted the wailing baby into her arms. She covered it partially with her own coat, and began running from house to house, to search for the baby's parents. The houses changed from split-levels to old colonials, and Pamela realized with terror that she no longer knew where she was. She ran to each front door, using doorknockers and doorbells, yelling for help to no avail. No one answered the doors, no one claimed the child. The infant had stopped crying, and Pamela looked down to check on her. It was at this point that Pamela was horrified by the blood collecting on her coat from the baby's injury. The door in front of her was her only hope. She knocked loudly, and finally the door became slightly ajar. Brian's face peered out at her, she screamed, and the infant took its last breath in her arms.

Pamela awoke with a start, her neck drenched with sweat and her heart beating wildly. That felt so real, she thought. She tried to calm herself by taking deep breaths and told herself to put the dream out of her mind. Maybe she would mention it on Thursday, to Rachel. She knew it had something to do with the abortion. That was obvious. Pamela started crying again, acknowledging to herself that she had no idea her decision would have caused this much agony. She had other friends, Tracy at work and Emily from high school, who had had abortions. She supported their decisions. She even helped with transportation to the clinic appointment for Emily. But this was more personal than political for Pamela. There was some profound reason for her agony, separate but connected to her own choices. Pamela resolved to try to tell Rachel; maybe she would help her to figure it out. Pamela was breathing regularly now. She managed to close her eyes and sleep soundly through the rest of the night.

※ ※

Pamela arrived at work early, said good morning to Tracy and Mr. Hansen, and noticed almost immediately that her ability to concentrate had improved. She thought about telling Mr. Hansen that she had followed through with his suggestion, but decided against it. I'll let him see the change in my work, she reasoned. Pamela pushed herself to finish much of the paperwork that had been neglected over the past several weeks, and felt proud of herself as she handed Mr. Hansen numerous letters she had typed. Mr. Hansen added his signature to them, and smiled warmly at Pamela as he said, "Please see that these go out today."

Pamela had the opportunity to talk with Tracy privately in the employee lounge at lunchtime. Tracy had seen Pamela enter Mr. Hansen's office for their private meeting, and was curious. Mr. Hansen usually met with both young women together. "Is everything okay with you, Pam?", she asked.

Tracy often gave Pamela 'the update', as she called it. Pamela was a good listener, and Tracy had shared many stories with her about her guy troubles. Pamela never judged her and Tracy appreciated that. She didn't give advice, either. Tracy wished she could do the same for her friend, but Pamela rarely talked about her personal life.

"Everything's okay, I've just been tired lately," Pamela reported.

"Because you seem kinda down…" Tracy abruptly stopped mid-sentence when several other women entered the lounge. Pamela and Tracy greeted them and began eating their lunches. Mrs. Falk was discussing her son's progress this semester at college with Mrs. Andersen. Both women had children Pamela's age. Mrs. Falk's son attended Tufts, and Mrs. Andersen's daughter was at Boston University.

College scared Pamela. She enjoyed working, and was not confident that she could work and attend college successfully. Her grades in high school had been okay, until senior year, when all the problems with Brian started. I never gave much thought to a career, Pamela pondered. I wish I could figure out what to do with my life.

Pamela was much less nervous when she arrived at Access Health Center on Thursday evening for her second appointment with Rachel. Rachel was wearing a plaid suit of earth tones and an olive green silk blouse. Pamela admired the outfit to herself. She once again followed Rachel to her office, and took a seat on the couch.

"How are you doing today, Pamela?"

Even Rachel's voice was soothing. "A little better, I think. I had a nightmare a few nights ago, though."

"What do you remember about it?"

Pamela discussed the details of her dream to the best of her ability. Rachel seemed very interested in the dream, and nodded as Pamela spoke. Pamela felt her nervousness return as she recounted the part about the baby's blood on her coat, her surprise at seeing Brian's face, and the infant's death in her arms. "I think the end is kind of obvious", she told Rachel. "I think the dream is about my…abortion." Pamela had not said the word before and it made her uncomfortable to use it now. Pamela felt like she was inside-out, very exposed, but pushed herself to go on. "I think there's more, though, was all she could say.

"Do you want to talk about it?"

"I'll try. I just think that something doesn't make sense. I know other people have done what I did, and I don't have a problem with it. But with me…well, it's different."

"In what way?"

"Like when I compare myself, I don't measure up."

"Compare yourself to whom?

"I don't know. I'm talking in circles. I can't figure it out. But there is something else I wanted to tell you today, before I forget. When you were asking me about my family on Monday, I wanted to tell you that I'm adopted. I was so upset about Brian that I forgot to mention it. Not that it matters. Sorry to change the subject." Pamela noticed Rachel nodding again.

"I'm not sure you have changed the subject."

"What do you mean?"

"I mean that maybe there's a connection between your adoption and your abortion."

"I'm sorry, I'm not following you."

"Pamela, correct me if I'm wrong about this, okay? But it seems to me that the person you might be comparing yourself with is your birth mother."

Pamela felt a chill run through her entire body. She knew Rachel was right. That was it! If her birth mother had chosen abortion, Pamela wouldn't be sitting here. "That's why I think I'm a bad person!" Pamela exclaimed. "I'm bad in comparison to my birth mother's choice to give me up for adoption! It's so odd, though, I never really thought much about being adopted before all this happened. But that's part of what makes me different. Oh, my goodness! I think that's why the houses changed in the dream!"

"Now it's my turn to ask what you mean."

"The houses went from split-levels to colonials, and I didn't recognize the street. In my mind, I had already made the connection! The scene changed from the present to the past. The infant changed to an injured baby without a home, and I couldn't find its parents. The dream was about abortion and adoption."

"That's very insightful, Pamela."

It was rare that Pamela received a compliment about her intelligence or insight. She did not respond to it. Rachel was impressed with Pamela's introspective ability. She decided to take another risk with Pamela. "Are there other ways you feel different because you were adopted?"

"Well, the usual ways, I guess. No one in my family looks like me. I was raised Jewish because my mother is Jewish, but I don't think I'm Jewish. The adoption was through Catholic Charities. There are more pictures of my brother growing up than there are of me. It was never very comfortable talking about my adoption, although my father told me when I was four years old. He read me a book about it, he was very open and honest, and he said they chose me because I was special. I love my father a lot." Pamela's tears began to flow again as she completed her sentence about her father. She reached for a tissue.

"Do you want to talk about what made you sad?"

"Well, what you said last time about the losses. I think I worry about rejection. Even though I know my father loves me, I always feel like if people really get to know me, they will reject me."

"Do you think you keep yourself from being known, in order to feel safe from rejection?"

"I'm not sure…"

"You mentioned that when you were with Brian, you deferred to him about decision-making. And judging from the acute pain you were in on Monday, I have a strong feeling you hadn't spoken with anyone about your troubles."

"You're right. I don't trust too many people, I do keep my problems to myself. And I let other people make decisions, because I don't really have any opinions of my own."

"I don't believe that."

"No, really, I have no opinions."

"Do you think Clinton should leave office?"

"Well, no, but I don't agree with what he did." Pamela thought about lying, how easy it was for her to lie if the alternative was to be discovered. She did have her share of secrets from people. She felt some kinship with the President. "I think he's doing a good job."

"Well, that's an opinion. Tell me some others."

"I think Clinton is a good President for the environment. I do worry about the water, and air pollution, and animals becoming extinct. I hate that animals are used in experiments. Actually, I was thinking that someday I might want to do something in that field, but I don't know much about it."

"Would you like to know more?"

"I would. My father wants me to go to college for something, maybe I could take some courses in Environmental Biology."

Rachel reached over to her bookshelf and handed a book to Pamela. "You can borrow this if you like."

The book was called *Living Downstream*, by Sandra Steingraber. Rachel had recently finished it, and thought of it as a sequel to Rachel Carson's Silent Spring. It contained information that would educate Pamela about the current environmental crisis, and she found it to be well written and easy to follow.

"Thanks," Pamela responded, "I'd like to borrow it."

Rachel glanced over at the clock on the wall. "Looks like our time is up for today, Pamela. When would you like to schedule our next meeting?"

"Monday would be good. " Pamela said. Rachel had given her plenty to think about for the weekend.

I have opinions, Pamela thought to herself as she drove past Brian's street on her way home. She was astounded as she admitted to herself that Brian never really knew her, and that perhaps she had wanted it that way. How can people care about you if they hardly know you? Maybe it was best that Brian broke off their contact. Maybe she would have time to focus on herself for a change, instead of worrying about

Brian all the time. "It's your loss!" Pamela shouted out her car window at Brian's garage door, almost believing it.

When Pamela arrived home, she discovered that her father had brought pizza for dinner, and it was still warm. Although her mother had many dietary restrictions, and had to be careful about fluid gains, she was enjoying a slice of pizza and a Coke. Pamela remembered talking to the nutritionist at Pioneer Valley Renal Center, and knew that there was something in the Coke that was bad for her mother, because her kidneys couldn't filter it out. She couldn't remember what the substance was, and thought she remembered that cheese was not so healthy either. But Pamela held her tongue and acted pleasant, knowing that nothing she said would influence her mother anyway. Perhaps Pamela perceived that she had no opinions because in this household, they didn't matter. Pamela sat down and joined her family at the formica kitchen table which had originally belonged to her father's parents. She cleared a space for her plate and helped herself to some pizza.

"Have you been working late at the office, Pammy?"

Her mother always called her Pammy. She hated it. And she realized that she was faced at this moment with an opportunity to stop the lying. To take more control in her life. Could she do it? "No." was all she could volunteer.

"We haven't seen Brian around here lately, were you visiting over there?"

"No."

Her mother sighed. Mrs. Roberta Windsor had tried for years to understand her daughter's withdrawal. It seemed that Pammy stopped talking to her when she approached adolescence. It was frightening how little she knew about her daughter's life, her whereabouts, all the changes she must be coping with alone. She knew she was to blame for some of their vicious arguments, and she vowed to stop being so critical of her daughter. Sometimes it was hard to watch this beautiful young woman she hardly knew, so poised and graceful in her movements, in perfect health, doing the work that her mother should be doing. Roberta thought of her own mother, also on dialysis for many years. Her mother was in her sixties now, and she often advised Roberta to be evaluated for a kidney transplant. Roberta's mother was on the transplant list in Florida, where she lived. Roberta was afraid of the surgery, and of the medications afterwards, which were immunosuppressants. Some of the patients she knew had been thrilled with their transplants, some had trouble with the medications or complications as a result of them. Either way, Roberta's kidneys had failed and she knew she had to stop projecting her anger onto her family. Especially Pamela. Roberta was concerned about her daughter's relationship with Brian. He was pleasant enough, but he was very immature, and Roberta was afraid that he had influenced her daughter not to consider college. He seemed only to care about his job and his car. Roberta had held back from speaking to Pamela about Brian, for she knew her dislike for him would only thrust her daughter further into his arms. She was shocked to hear what Pamela whispered.

"I'm not seeing him anymore."

"What happened?"

"We broke up. I was upset about it at first, but now I think it's for the best."

"Oh, Pammy, I'm sorry. I wish you felt like you could talk to me about these things."

"It's not just you, Mom. I don't talk to anyone." Pamela tried to focus on the caring she heard in her mother's voice. She could be very warm, like she was sometimes before she got ill. "In fact, I started seeing a counselor last week."

"Do you really think you need to, honey?"

"Well, I think it's helping me. I have to try to figure out some stuff, Mom."

"What are you trying to figure out, Pamela?" her father interjected, between bites of pizza.

"She just wants us all to know that she doesn't know anything!" her brother Robert hissed.

Pamela ignored him. "I like my job, but I don't want to be an administrative assistant all my life. I'm thinking about going to college."

Pamela's parents exchanged glances, and she knew they were thrilled to hear her say something about college. They had thought she had made an error last September in not enrolling, and as February approached, she knew they had concerns that she would not apply again this year.

"That's wonderful, Pamela. We're glad to hear it!" her father announced. "You know I'll help you with the tuition, honey. Your mother and I think you'll be terrific at anything you choose to do."

"Yeah, right." Robert added sarcastically.

"Thanks, Dad." Pamela had said more than she had planned. What if I don't get accepted to a college, she asked herself. How will I work and go to school? What if it's too hard for me? I don't want to disappoint them, she thought. And in that instant, she understood her fears about college. She heard Rachel's voice in her mind. *Keeping yourself safe from rejection.* And Pamela understood in that moment her decision not to decide. She hadn't applied to school or thought about a career because of her fear of not being accepted, of not being good enough. Now she had to try.

Pamela cleared the table after dinner, gathered her belongings, and retreated to her room. Her parents and brother watched television in the living room. She reached for Living Downstream and read the book jacket about the author. Once she began reading, the book held her interest, and she felt as if she was absorbing the information like a sponge. It was almost 10:00p.m. when her father knocked on her door.

"Just wanted to say goodnight, honey. And please let us help you out with applying to colleges, okay? You made me very happy tonight. What are you reading?"

"A book about the environment. It's called Living Downstream. It's very good. Overwhelming, but good."

This was the first time that Nelson Windsor had ever seen his daughter engrossed in something other than a romance novel. Not that he had anything against Rosamunde Pilcher, but he was aware that his daughter thought of herself as less capable than she was. He wondered if this belief kept her from reading non-fiction. And from college as well, for that matter. He was stumped about Pamela's low self-esteem. He tried to love her as well as he knew how. He had been a good provider. Well, he thought, tonight he had a glimpse of a side of her he hoped to get to know better. As he kissed his daughter goodnight, he had the distinct feeling he detected the scent of a small yellow rose whose petals were opening to fullness.

Chapter 3

On Saturday morning, Pamela decided to visit the West Springfield Library. She spent time exploring the reference section, and perused several college catalogs that were stocked with information about environmental careers. Some colleges offered internships at agencies dealing with ecological concerns. Pamela found that she was filled with enthusiasm about applying to some of these colleges, and she spent hours investigating her choices. Pamela had also brought Living Downstream along with her, and read several chapters in the comfort of the library. Before she left, Pamela discovered a book written by Al Gore when he was a senator, entitled *Earth in the Balance* which she checked out at the library counter.

Her next stop was the post office, where Pamela purchased postcards. Pamela had jotted down demographics about a few schools of interest, and sent postcards to each college so that applications would begin to arrive at her home. She returned home with a smile on her face, and her mother greeted her, letting her know that Tracy had phoned and would like a call back.

Pamela called Tracy from her bedroom for privacy.
"Hello?"
"Hi, Tracy, it's Pam."
"Hi! I didn't get a chance to talk to you at lunch the other day. Do you have any time this weekend for us to get together?"

"I have all the time in the world, Tracy. I'm not seeing Brian anymore. In fact, he broke up with me weeks ago. I just didn't feel like talking about it until now."

"Wow, I'm sorry. You really loved him."

"I thought I did. But you know something? I'm realizing that it wasn't the greatest with him. I can honestly say I don't miss him so much anymore."

"Well, I just had a fight with Jason, if it makes you feel any better."

"We deserve better, Tracy, I'm starting to believe that. Anyway, I just came from the library. I'm thinking of applying for college this fall."

"Cool! That's great! Where are you thinking of going?"

"Why don't I come over with the information? Are you free tonight?"

"Sure!"

"Great! Bye!"

Pamela ate dinner with her family, adding to the conversation in an unusual manner, and discussing her newfound knowledge about global warming, ecosystems, tropical rain forests, recycling and waste disposal. Her brother was so astounded that he ate with his mouth agape, as if he hardly recognized her. He's disgusting, Pamela thought. Her father played devil's advocate in his lawyerly way, and Pamela found herself capable of debating his arguments and holding her own ground. Pamela's mother, surprisingly, was supportive of each point Pamela made. Pamela had mentioned the catalogs at dinner as well, and promised to share her ideas with her parents on Sunday, after talking things over with Tracy.

She left the house and headed north on Route 5 to Holyoke, where Tracy lived with her parents and sisters. Tracy shared a room with one of her sisters. When Pamela arrived, Tracy suggested that they drive to the nearby Friendly's for some ice cream and privacy. Pamela carried her library information to the passenger side of Tracy's blue Toyota Tercel, and they drove the short distance to the restaurant together. Tracy asked Pamela to elaborate on her last few days with Brian, and Tracy spoke about Jason as well. Once seated inside Friendly's, Pamela changed the subject and discussed her concerns about college with her friend.

Pamela was honest with Tracy about her fears about being accepted to college, and she realized as she spoke that Brian had escalated those fears. Being called an idiot never did much toward enhancing Pamela's already low opinion of herself. Tracy related an incident with Jason which proved that she could empathize with Pamela about being ridiculed as well. Pamela asked if Tracy had ever thought about a career, and Tracy answered that she dreamed of having her own business someday. Tracy had a strong fashion sense and loved crafts and home décor. Pamela knew that Tracy was also good with numbers from the bookkeeping assistance she gave to the accountant at work. Pamela tried to be encouraging. She realized this conversation was embarking on new territory, both in terms of the information shared and the type of communication between them. Pamela started to address the notion of leaving Massachusetts to attend school. One of the most interesting catalogs Pamela had seen was from the University of Colorado at Boulder. The pictures in the catalog looked beautiful, mountainous and scenic like Route 91 North to Northampton and Vermont, but more awesome. And the curriculum sounded really interesting. Pamela had traveled to most of the New England states, but had never been anywhere else in the country. There was also a school in New England called Antioch, in Keene, New Hampshire. Pamela's dilemma about leaving home had a lot to do with her parents. How would her mother function without her help? And how would she survive living on her own without her father nearby?

Tracy was encouraging, although she admitted that she would miss Pamela if she left the area. Tracy offered an unexpected suggestion. How about taking a vacation to Boulder, to see the area and help Pamela decide? Pamela loved the idea, but financing the trip would be difficult for both of them. Once their desserts arrived, the young women savored them, and settled into a discussion about work.

That evening, Pamela arrived home after 10:00 o'clock, and found a note taped to her bedroom door. Brian had called! Pamela's heart seemed to occupy her throat, and she caught her breath without uttering a sound. Last week, she thought, I would have been thrilled to get a message from him. Now, my heart is pounding and I'm anxious again. I don't even know if I should call back. Well, there's no emergency, I can sleep on it, Pamela decided. And then, after retiring to bed, Pamela changed her mind. I will not call him back. I'm angry about how he treated me. I don't want to put myself in that situation again. Pamela sighed heavily, closed her eyes, and imagined hiking in the Rocky Mountains with Tracy.

* * * * * * * * * * * * * * * * * *

On Sunday, Pamela broke the news to her parents about the catalogs that would be arriving from New Hampshire and Colorado. They handled the news better than she had anticipated, and they discussed the obstacles involved together. Her brother, who was playing a computer game in the study, participated in his selfish way as well. He eavesdropped on their conversation from the study, and interrupted. "Hey, Pamela, if you get into school, you're gonna leave me your car, right?"

Pamela's Aunt Maxine, her mother's sister, was in the midst of a divorce. Her mother suggested that they offer Aunt Maxine a place to stay for a while after the divorce, rent-free, if she would consider helping around the house. Of course, this arrangement would mean that Pamela would have to forfeit her bedroom, but she was open to the idea. She was thinking of the relief she would have if she only had herself to consider, and for the first time, Pamela's guilt about leaving turned to excitement.

On Monday, Pamela told Rachel all of her news. It seemed odd, she acknowledged, that so many things were happening so fast. Pamela discussed the books she had been reading, her growing interest in an environmental career, her trip to the library, her conversation with Tracy, and her discussion with her parents. She also mentioned Brian's phone call, and was proud to tell Rachel that she had decided not to call back. Pamela embarked on a conversation about her relationship with Brian that detailed his treatment of her. She spoke of the one time he had hit her. Brian had said she was irritating him, and told her to stop asking stupid questions. Absentmindedly, Pamela asked Brian something minutes later, and Brian slapped her across the face. Pamela had felt her lip begin to bleed, and the swelling was hard to hide the next day. Pamela spoke about that incident, and others, without tears this time. And she realized as she spoke that Rachel was right. She hadn't deserved to be hit. Perhaps it was over with her and Brian for real.

Pamela also discussed her fears about leaving home, and became more confident that a trip to Colorado might be in order. It would help her to decide, as Tracy had suggested. Pamela had vacation time at work, and she decided that she would explore the idea, call some airlines and check on ticket prices. Her father belonged to an automobile club, and she would be able to order some booklets about the area to check into hotels as well. Just in case she was accepted. She would await the arrival of the catalog, complete the application, and if she received an acceptance letter, Pamela would plan her trip. It felt good to have a goal, Pamela told Rachel.

When Pamela left Access Health Services, she walked toward the old brick building where the Catholic Charities office was. I finally have something to tell my birth mother, Pamela thought. Something good that I'm trying to accomplish. I wonder if she thinks about me. If she would even want to know about my life. Pamela stood motionless in front of the building that held her birth records. She was paralyzed by her ambivalence about searching for her birth mother. Pamela made a mental note to really talk to Rachel about her adoption concerns, and backtracked to her Hyundai, heading to the only home she had ever known.

Chapter 4

Rachel's caseload was expanding at Access Health Center. On Monday nights, she worked late into the evening. Her schedule prevented her from spending much time during the week with her husband, Glen Moss. Glen was accustomed to cooking dinner for himself, and would reheat a portion for Rachel when she arrived home.

Rachel and Glen lived in a condominium complex in Northampton. The grounds were tastefully landscaped and the one-bedroom condominium was large enough to accommodate their lifestyle. The couple had been married four years ago, and they were saving their money to purchase a home. Glen worked as a supervisor for a telemarketing firm in Hadley. He enjoyed his work, but was always glad to be coming home. Glen considered himself a humanitarian, and did not feel intimidated by the fact that Rachel had more education and a higher income than he did. He felt proud of his wife, and knew she would be able to help many people during the course of her chosen career. He was concerned about Rachel lately, though, because of her long hours. It seemed that her work at Access Health Center was exhausting at times, and as a result, Rachel had less energy for their relationship.

Glen's philosophy about work was very different than Rachel's. Glen worked in order to have the money to play. He loved travel, skiing and photography, and spent a good deal of his income on his interests. Work was simply the means by which he was able to enjoy himself. Rachel thought of work very differently. Work to Glen's wife was more like a mission, giving life its purpose and enhancing Rachel's self-esteem. Rachel felt that one should always utilize one's talents in choosing a profession. She took her work very seriously, and never seemed to be bothered by the fact that there was practically no time off. Now that she was working full-time at Access Health Center, Rachel's responsibilities also included an on-call rotation. To Glen, this meant occasional restless nights attempting to fall asleep following a crisis call. He would listen to Rachel's soft voice counseling a stranger threatening suicide, and wonder why in the world anyone would choose the field of social work as a profession. Rachel did not discuss her work with Glen, informing him that she was mandated to hold people's conversations in confidence. Although Rachel thought Glen would be offended when this issue came to the surface, in reality, he didn't care to know about her clients at all. He just wished his wife could learn to relax and enjoy herself a bit, as her long hours and responsibilities seemed to exhaust her. Not that Rachel complained; she never did.

Glen wasn't so fond of being analytical, but he wondered if Rachel sometimes used her work to distance herself from him. After all, she had her reasons for needing distance. Prior to their wedding, Rachel had insisted that Glen attend several therapy sessions along with Rachel and her counselor, Barbara Nathanson. Glen sat in the therapy room with these two women, one he was about to marry, and one he hardly knew. He rarely participated. He remembered Rachel talking about her fears about being married, including her concern that she would not be able to balance her fierce need for independence with her need for intimacy. Rachel had been in a few other relationships, and had told Glen that in each one, she eventually lost her attraction for the person, and 'fell out of love'. She didn't want this to happen with Glen, and became tearful as she told him so. Glen reached for Rachel's hand in front of Barbara Nathanson, announcing that it was his opinion she simply hadn't met the right man – until now.

After that session, he was told he was 'minimizing' Rachel's concerns. Rachel felt things very deeply, and often felt misunderstood. He didn't mean to minimize, he explained, but simply to express his love for her, and his hope that this relationship would be different—and better—for Rachel than the others had been. Rachel could be very nurturing. Glen enjoyed her generosity. Rachel was generous with her words as well as her deeds. She would often arrive home with something special for her husband, wrapped with extra care, even though there was no occasion to celebrate. Glen had opened many gifts from Rachel. Each time, he stared down into a box of something familiar. Rachel seemed to memorize and record each shopping venture they took together, noticing the items Glen paid special attention to, and returning to purchase them at some later date. And each gift came with a card, to which Rachel had added some poetry of her own. Apparently, Glen made Rachel feel safe, and this feeling was the basis for much of her poetry. Glen had no idea how he created safety for his wife. He knew he was easygoing and articulate about many subjects, maybe even fun to be with. He had a good sense of humor, and Rachel often laughed at his jokes. He suspected that for his introspective wife, however, safety came from sources other than superficial traits. He suspected that for Rachel, safety came from knowing Glen would never intentionally hurt her.

Rachel had told Glen early in their courtship that she had been abused as a child. She spoke mostly about physical abuse, but Glen had assumed there was more. Rachel had postponed sexual intimacy in their relationship for a long time, and when she finally became comfortable with the idea of making love, she could only do so under certain circumstances. The lights had to be on. Rachel had to remove her own clothing. Some types of foreplay would provoke tears. Glen would speak softly to Rachel, pledging his love and holding back until Rachel took control of their lovemaking. Once she did so, it seemed to Glen that she transitioned from childlike to adult, and her intensity was like nothing Glen had ever known. She would caress his muscular body, and love him tenderly with no inhibitions, intent on satisfying him sexually with little interest in her own pleasure. It was months before Glen realized that Rachel rarely allowed herself to travel to the heights that she would take him. And it was years before Rachel told him that she had never been able to climax during lovemaking. She never said the words sexual abuse. But as far as Glen was concerned, she didn't have to.

Rachel pulled her Volkswagen into her usual parking spot, and Glen heard the familiar sound of her car puttering to a stop. The car was ten years old, and sounded more like a lawn mower to Glen's ears than an automobile. Rachel loved that car, though, and Glen certainly couldn't offer to replace it on his income. Glen walked to the window, and noticed that Rachel carried her briefcase in one hand and a package in the other. Another gift, he thought. Glen opened the front door for his wife as she approached.

"Hi, honey, you look beat!" Glen kissed his wife and helped her with her things. He glanced at his watch and saw that it was already ten o'clock.

"And I'm on call tonight, but it's a weeknight, it should be quiet."

"Did you eat? I made pasta primavera if you want some."

"That sounds great, Glen, I'll just wash up and be out in a minute. I'm starved!"

Glen joined Rachel at the table in their eat-in kitchen. He removed Rachel's dinner after heating it in the microwave, and set it in front of her. "What do you want to drink?"

"Just water, thanks. How was your day?"

Glen spoke about the two new students he had hired to work as telemarketers. He was hopeful that they would both stay around awhile, as his firm had a good deal of staff turnover. As usual, Rachel said little about her day at work. Glen thought she looked troubled as he glanced into her tired, hazel eyes.

"I have something for you, Glen. I almost forgot!"

"What is it?"

"Open it and see."

Glen opened the small package and saw the flash attachment he had examined last month in the camera store in the Holyoke Mall. "It's perfect for my old Olympus camera, honey, thank you. You always know exactly what I want." Glen had an Olympus OM-1 that was no longer made, but still took great photographs. The flash was used, but in very good condition. Glen made a mental note to try it out this weekend.

"I'm glad you like it." Rachel looked satisfied with her purchase. She finished her meal and stood to wash her plate in the sink. "Any news about the impeachment hearings?"

"Some senators are talking about a motion to dismiss. Can you believe it?"

"I hope it passes. I'm going to watch the news for a while, if I can keep my eyes open."

"I'll join you."

Glen and Rachel watched the news in silence. Glen massaged Rachel's shoulders briefly. He decided to inquire about his observation of earlier. "Is anything wrong, Rachel?"

"No, why do you ask?"

"You seem far away tonight. Not very talkative."

"I'm just pensive, I guess. I'm treating a new patient who reminds me a little of myself. She's nineteen, with a very promising future, but she doesn't think much of herself."

"You don't have to tell me about this…"

"No, it's okay, I won't mention names. I've just been thinking about her because her adolescence sounds a bit like mine was. Her father is no ogre, though."

Glen knew that Rachel was referring to her abuse again. "Well, I guess she's luckier than you were. Is your aim to help her to feel better about herself, like you say Barbara has helped you?"

"I hope I can do that. She may be leaving in September, so I don't have much time."

Glen patted his wife's hand. "You'll be able to help her, I know it."

Rachel smiled, and they retired to the bedroom arm in arm, both knowing that Rachel had too much on her mind to consider anything but sleep.

Chapter 5

On her drive to work the next morning, Rachel encountered black ice on Route 91 South. She was an overly cautious driver, and reduced her speed just enough to irritate other drivers. Rachel daydreamed about winters on Long Island, where she grew up. Although most of the memories of her childhood were bleak, Rachel missed the warmer winters and the ocean beaches. Rachel had decided to move to Massachusetts, and had no regrets about doing so. Getting away from her father helped Rachel immensely, and she had chosen to have no contact with him since she left nineteen years ago. Rachel was an only child. Her mother was diagnosed with uterine cancer when Rachel was nine years old. Janine Andrews Abbott was a loving woman, concerned about her only daughter until her death in 1978. The cancer reduced her mother's ability to care for herself during the last year of her life. Rachel acted as caregiver at home, and coordinated a group of her mother's friends to drive to doctor's appointments. Her father was seldom available.

Janine Abbott chose to die in her own home, with hospice care. Rachel was by her side when her mother took her last breath. The nurse had left them alone for a few minutes, and although her mother was drugged to dissipate her pain, she managed to clearly express herself to Rachel. "I'll be watching over you," was the statement Rachel distinctly remembered. At the end, Janine Abbott apologized to her daughter.

"I'm sorry, Rachel," she whispered. "I don't think I can fight anymore." "I love you, Mom," was Rachel's response. She had shed so many tears about her mother's illness that her eyes were dry. Rachel's head hurt. The nurse returned and hugged Rachel, telling her she was very brave, and that her mother loved her very much.

Rachel tried to keep her emotions in check, attending school and focusing on her homework, distracting herself from her grief. She started making lists of chores, lists of groceries, lists of everything. Rachel began to straighten up her closet, putting her clothes in color order from dark to light, and doing the same with her drawers of socks and underclothes. Her father gave her a key to the house, so she could let herself in after school. At least he's not fighting with her anymore, Rachel thought. Rachel's parents argued loudly enough to wake her from a sound sleep. Before her mother was too weak to stand, the fights would sometimes end with a pot banging or a phone flying, the sound of a wall being punched or a door being slammed. Rachel hated her father for yelling at her mother. She had crept downstairs to intervene when she was smaller, but she had learned her lesson. His fists would fly in her direction just as easily as they would her mother's. Rachel would have to coexist with him for years before she could leave, and she was always getting headaches whenever she thought about that.

Brendon Abbott was not able to communicate with his daughter. He was distraught after his wife's death, and left his daughter to fend for herself. His drinking escalated, and he would sometimes awaken on the living room couch, yelling that Rachel should be quieter as she prepared for school. He seemed to have little memory of the night before.

But Rachel remembered. And she became furious at her mother for dying. "You said you'd watch over me," she would demand of her mother's photograph. "Why are you letting him hurt me? Make him stop!" Rachel was repulsed at the intrusive image she remembered next. Her father had called her by her mother's name, drunk and slobbering on top of her.

Rachel's Volkswagen hit another patch of black ice, and she realized she had missed her exit. Rachel saw signs for Enfield, Connecticut, and had to turn around at the next possible exit to return to Springfield. She was late for her first client, and Rachel arrived in a panic. She rushed through the door to the Health Center's waiting room, and was relieved to discover that her client was not there yet. Hilary handed Rachel a message from the client. He was late due to the weather, but was on his way.

Rachel had several cancellations in the afternoon, and found herself daydreaming about Glen. I wonder how much he knows about my father. I'm so lucky to have found a man who can be so patient and understanding. Glen intuitively gave her control over situations that were difficult for her sexually. He amazed her. Somehow, he managed to help her to keep her flashbacks out of the bedroom. She hadn't had one flashback during their lovemaking in the past four years! That was a miracle. Rachel had worked hard in therapy to re-experience the terror of her father's abuse, with the hope of closing the door to her trauma history. She was finally seeing some results, and her marriage was proof that Rachel could lead a normal life. It was a good marriage. Rachel sighed, eyeing the paperwork on her desk.

Rachel completed several outpatient treatment reports for various insurance companies. Pamela Windsor's treatment report was next in the pile. Rachel diagnosed Pamela with a mild form of Adjustment Disorder. Pamela did not meet full criteria for another diagnosis, and suffered from alternating depression and anxiety as a result of her recent losses. Otherwise, Pamela was a high-functioning adolescent who was coping with the normal life tasks for her age. An identity crisis, exacerbated by her recent abortion, and her concerns about adoption. Rachel conjectured that Pamela might be considering searching for her birth family. She sympathized with Pamela. It was difficult enough to explore one's identity without having an additional family to consider. Brian's breaking up with her on her birthday may also have triggered thoughts about the initial rejection inherent in her adoption. And because of her fragile definition of herself, Pamela was especially vulnerable to self-criticism after her abortion. Unfortunately, Rachel knew that self-criticism all too well.

Barbara Nathanson knew about Rachel's abortion. And her father, of course, and the doctor that her father paid to perform it. The abortion was unbearable for Rachel to think about. She had waited a long time to tell anyone, and she was only thirteen years old when she realized she was gaining weight. Rachel had just begun to menstruate and had not been recording the dates of her periods. It was her homeroom teacher that Rachel told. Her homeroom teacher called the school psychologist, and Rachel met with Mrs. Miller at first period instead of going to study hall for a few weeks. Mrs. Miller asked about Rachel's friend, Neil. She asked personal questions that Rachel had trouble answering. Rachel had not had sex with Neil. They were just friends, and he would sometimes take her to a movie with his older brother, Jordan. Rachel and Neil were both good students, often ostracized from the class because it seemed to take little effort for their grades to be superior. They related to each other as outcasts, and bookworms who would often study together prior to exams. School was Rachel's haven after her mother's death. Her teachers were fond of her. Her homeroom teacher, Miss Engels, always took a special interest in Rachel. Miss Engels had noticed that Rachel had been gaining weight after her mother's death, but assumed that she was eating more as a way of coping with her grief. Rachel lived in a kind of netherworld after her mother's body was buried. She was dissociated, lost, focusing only on her schoolwork and pushing the knowledge of her father's abuse as far back in her mind as it would retreat. Some days, she was more successful than others. Rachel knew that Miss Engels and Mrs. Miller would never suspect her father of rape. They would go on assuming that Rachel was promiscuous and had been having sexual intercourse with Neil. Rachel felt awful about condemning Neil indirectly, but she could not bring herself to tell the truth about her father. If she told her secret and was believed, she didn't know what would happen to her father or where she would live. If she told and was not believed, she didn't know what her father would do to her. She had witnessed too much violence to trust him. Rachel was paralyzed by her fears, and kept silent for several months after acknowledging her condition. She was confused as well, because she would occasionally discover blood in her underclothes. If she were pregnant, why would she be bleeding? She learned in Health Education that menstruation ceases with pregnancy. Rachel yearned for her mother's comfort.

Mrs. Miller told Rachel about residences that took pregnant teens under their wings. If she were accepted into a residence, she would have to relocate until her baby was due. Because Rachel was still a minor, she would have to get her father's approval for the placement. She would be able to finish the school year and move during the summer. Mrs. Miller had done some research, and had found that there was a bed available in a residence in Suffolk County. She would have to be interviewed, with her father present, within the next week. Mrs. Miller could schedule the date and time, but Rachel would have to confront her father with the news. Mrs. Miller offered to be available to Rachel if she wanted to invite her father to the school, but that option felt too dangerous to her.

Rachel had difficulty standing when it was time to leave Mrs. Miller's office. Her pants were sticking to her thighs, and her legs were shaking. She calmed herself by pretending she was with her mother, walking along Jones Beach, instead of walking the hallways of the school. She distracted herself during her classes and left school early, feigning illness.

On the walk home from school, Rachel felt her baby's kick. She had felt something similar before, but this was much stronger, more persistent. Her eyes widened and she tried to act nonchalant, hoping simultaneously that it would never happen again, and that it would happen again. Maybe I can get away from my father, have this baby, and go back to school, with help from the residence. But how would she manage to obtain her father's approval? She knew what she would have to do.

Rachel walked to Neil's house instead of going directly home. He answered her knock, and they sat on the porch, talking. Rachel told him the miserable details of her situation, and Neil grew angrier as she spoke. He wasn't in the least bit mad about his guilt by association. He was relieved that Rachel saw him as a cushion for her reality. Neil was angry that her father had the power to devastate Rachel in this way. Rachel's entire life would be affected by his crimes against her. First, her mother died, and now this, Neil thought. No wonder the light has left her eyes. Neil asked if there was anything he could do. He thought of asking his mother if Rachel could stay with them, but Rachel wanted only to be permitted to call her father from Neil's home. She would tell him her news over the telephone. She would pack some luggage when her father left for work and perhaps stay at Neil's for a while, if the residence did not accept her.

The plan failed. Rachel did speak to her father that night, and his speech was slurred. He had been drinking heavily, and Rachel was unsure as to whether or not he would remember their conversation. He was furious. He told her "You'll have that baby over my dead body!" and hung up the phone. Rachel decided to stay on Neil's living room couch, with his mother's permission. They told Neil's mother that she had had a fight with her father. In the morning, Neil lent Rachel one of his tee shirts. It was large and dark, and hid her stomach. She liked the feel of it and wore it to school.

Rachel had no idea what her father was capable of doing about her pregnancy. She understood she was a minor and he had the power to make all decisions. She was terribly shocked when she arrived home after school to pack her things, and discovered her father's car in the driveway. He must've stayed home from work, Rachel told herself.

Brendon Abbott had arranged to take his daughter to Manhattan for a doctor's appointment. He was calmer, and told Rachel she had to see an obstetrician if she wanted to consider having this baby. He's changed his mind, Rachel assumed, relieved. Her father was nervous, pacing the living room as he spoke.

"Do what you have to do, we're leaving in a few minutes."

Rachel took time to wash and change her clothing, and walked out of the house toward her father's car. He unlocked it, and they sat together wordlessly in the front seat. The drive seemed to take forever to Rachel. She hoped her father condemned her for having sex with Neil. She hoped he had no memory of the misery he caused in her bedroom. Maybe he really thought she was her mother. She had no way of knowing for sure.

The doctor's office was in a large hospital uptown. Rachel thought the doctor seemed irritated with her. It figures Dad would find someone like this to take care of me, Rachel thought, her fear mounting. The doctor examined Rachel for a long time. He poked and prodded and hurt her in ways that reminded her of her father's abuse. She allowed her mind to drift away, and imagined herself floating near the ceiling. She focused on the ceiling tiles, counting crevices, until the examination finally ended. The doctor spoke with her father privately for a long while. Rachel sat impatiently in the waiting area, staring at the door to the doctor's office. The brass plate on the door read Dr. Mark Russell. When the doctor returned with her father, Rachel remembered, her head began to ache. The horrible stabbing sensation continued around her temples. She was nauseous, and the florescent lights were bothering her eyes. She was led to a small room. Rachel's memory became very foggy about the events that followed. Rachel awoke in a small private room with a nurse by her bedside. She was still medicated and groggy. Her mouth was dry, but she was not thirsty. She was still nauseous, and her body had noticeably changed shape. The reasons for her hospital visit came flooding back to her. Rachel was miserable. Her father sat in the corner of the room, and explained to her that he had signed some paperwork allowing the doctors to perform a late-stage abortion. Rachel felt a scream forming in her throat, but as if in a nightmare, she could not make a sound. Tears rolled down her cheeks like a lazy river, flowing back toward her ears and jaw and down her neck as she lay absolutely still. I will never forgive him for this, Rachel told herself. And in that moment, she made a decision. She had nothing else to lose. Rachel mustered up her courage. She tried to imagine her mother standing beside her.

"This is all your fault," she announced to her father. "If you touch me again, I'll kill you."

Brendon Abbott stood, laughed sadistically, and left the room. Dr. Russell met him in the hallway, and they exchanged some words that Rachel could not hear. Dr. Russell seemed irritated with her father as well. The doctor entered Rachel's room, asked how she was feeling and told her she would be staying overnight at the hospital. When she was discharged the following day, Rachel's father was nowhere to be found. She checked her knapsack, and discovered some grocery money stashed in one of its compartments. Rachel had traveled to Manhattan enough with her mother to be aware of the city streets, and oriented herself when she arrived outside of the building. She began walking downtown, and made her way to Pennsylvania Station on 34th Street. Rachel took the escalator instead of the stairs, and remembered to look for signs for the Long Island Rail Road.

Rachel bought a ticket to the Wantagh station, and boarded the next train. I'll call Neil, maybe his brother will be home, Rachel thought. It was Saturday, and she arrived at dinnertime. Rachel found a pay phone.

"Hello?"

Neil's voice sounded like an angel's. "Neil, it's Rachel. I'm at Wantagh train station. My father never came to pick me up at the hospital. Is Jordan home? Can you pick me up?"

"Yes, he's home, and we were just heading out to McDonald's. It's across the street from the station. Can you meet us over there in about ten minutes?"

"Thanks, Neil, I'll be there."

"Rachel? Are you okay?"

"I'm better now than I was five minutes ago."

"OK, I'll see you soon."

Jordan and Neil treated Rachel to a hamburger, fries and a soda, and the food tasted much better than the hospital meals. Jordan kept the conversation light, and had them laughing about the antics of his fellow students at Wantagh High School. They drove past Rachel's house after dinner, and her father's car was gone. She ran inside to collect some personal things and a change of clothing. Neil had already gotten permission from his mother for Rachel to sleep on the couch again. When they arrived, though, Neil chivalrously forfeited his bedroom to Rachel, and after helping her with the school assignments she had missed, he slept on the couch that night.

In Neil's bed, Rachel looked up at the ceiling. "Mom," she whispered, "you know I can't go back there. I can't stay here. Please help me figure out what to do." Rachel conjured up a picture of her mother in her mind, and it was the image of her face that helped Rachel to sleep.

Her mother came to Rachel in her dream. It was just a normal day, like any day with her mother. Rachel accompanied her to Harborwood Shopping Center, and they went grocery shopping. Afterwards, Rachel asked her mother if they could stop at the bakery, her favorite place for sweets. Her mother bought Rachel a large butter cookie with chocolate sprinkles, and Rachel ate it with delight. They went home and cooked dinner together. Dinner was delicious, and Rachel washed the dishes afterwards. Rachel's mother was in her bedroom, and Rachel climbed the stairs to see her. Her mother was opening the top drawer of her bureau and closing it again. Over and over. She was verbalizing something that Rachel couldn't hear. When Rachel awoke from her dream, that was all she could remember. It had been soothing to dream of her mother. The dream comforted Rachel as she began preparing for school, and Neil and Rachel walked together, arriving on time.

There were plenty of whispers in the hallway that day. Just two more weeks until finals, Rachel assured herself. I'll make it. Then I'll figure out what I'm doing. She stopped at home after school to pack some luggage, gathering all her school texts in order to bring them to Neil's house. And then the dream came back to her.

Rachel headed upstairs into her parents' bedroom. Her father had left everything exactly as it had been before her mother died. Her mother's clothes were still hanging neatly on her side of the closet, and her jewelry box still held her small collection of valuables. Rachel walked over to her bureau. She opened the top drawer. There, in the corner, was her mother's address book. It was the address book that her mother had kept since Rachel was very small, and it was ragged and torn at the edges. Rachel put the address book in her knapsack. She took one of her mother's sweaters as well, and a heart necklace from her jewelry box that Rachel had always admired. It had a small ruby in the center of a gold heart that was surrounded by small diamonds. It had been given to Rachel's mother by her older sister, Rachel's Aunt Lynn. Rachel hadn't seen her Aunt Lynn in almost six years. Her mother had explained that she had had a big fight with her family. *Why does everyone fight with my mother?* Her maternal grandmother and her Aunt Lynn lived in a rural part of Massachusetts. Rachel used to visit them with her mother during the summer months. She hadn't thought of them in years. They never even came to her mother's funeral.

Rachel focused again on the insurance paperwork. It's amazing, she thought, how working with Pamela Windsor seems to trigger all this attention to my own past. It struck Rachel that she was especially drawn to Pamela, and she decided to discuss the dynamic with her supervisor. Rachel had seldom worked with adolescent clients, let alone clients whose lives paralleled her own. Obvious parallels aside, though, there seemed to be something special about her relationship with Pamela that reached beyond the scope of professional countertransference. In Rachel's wildest dreams, she could never have imagined how their lives would soon intertwine.

Chapter 6

Pamela received her college catalogs in the mail during the week, and was surprised by her level of motivation to write her personal essays. Pamela had always thought of herself as very reserved and shy. Yet, here she was, pondering how best to express her interests to strangers on admission committees with a confidence she had not experienced before.

The Antioch application procedure included an interview, and Pamela deliberated about asking her father to accompany her to New Hampshire. She would be very nervous, and would certainly feel more comfortable if her father went along. He might have to take time off from work, so Pamela would have to give him as much notice as possible. She looked down at her personal essay, which continued to take shape. I would like to learn as much as possible about solutions to our environmental problems, Pamela wrote, rather than allowing frustration and discouragement to inhibit my ability to take action. I believe that knowledge of the environmental crisis is crucial to my generation. Only knowledge will instill the power to gradually reverse our planet's at-risk status. I would appreciate the opportunity to obtain this knowledge at Antioch…

Pamela put her pen down. She was at work, and had taken some time to continue writing her essay. Mr. Hansen approached her, and she quickly manipulated some papers on her desk to appear as if she had been working on them.

"Pamela, I just wanted to say that I've noticed a big change in your work, and I'm very pleased."

Pamela smiled and felt incredibly guilty. Tracy looked over from her cubicle to acknowledge Pamela. She formed the words "Nice going" so that Pamela could read her lips. Pamela decided she would finish her essays at home. The middle of February was approaching, and there were time constraints. She would have to complete the essays as soon as possible and withdraw the money from her checking account for the application fees. Pamela noticed the clock on the wall over her desk. It was nearly time to leave work for the day. She would soon be talking to Rachel again at Access Health Center.

"A few weeks ago, I walked by Catholic Charities," Pamela told Rachel. "I couldn't bring myself to enter the building, but I did feel like I finally have something I'd like to share with my birth mother. Maybe she'd be proud of me, I don't know. I don't know why she gave me up. I was told that she got pregnant very young. I wonder if she was a minor. Maybe her parents made the decision. Who knows? I wonder if it was even her choice."

Rachel felt small beads of sweat forming on the back of her neck. *If she were a minor, her parents could make that decision for her.*

"I might have grandparents, too!" Pamela verbalized her thought aloud. "And a brother or sister somewhere…I think I want to try to find them."

"Let's talk about your expectations."

"Well, I haven't thought about it too much. My fear always gets in the way. I guess I'm afraid of her rejecting me. You know, like I would go crazy trying to find her and then she won't want to know me. That would be really hard, I think. But I could still find out if I look like her or act like her. A search might help me to feel more grounded, even if she does reject me. Maybe she'll be willing to at least tell me about my ethnic background. And I do want to have my own family someday, more than anything. My own children. I could ask about medical histories of family members. I should know that information before having kids. I know where I was born, my date of birth, and my father told me her name once. It's Ann Kenney. My father called it an 'open adoption'. He told me that if I write to her through Catholic Charities, they'll send her the letter, and with her permission, Catholic Charities will send me her response. I've started writing about a thousand letters to her, but I've never had the nerve to send them."

Rachel could see the turmoil in Pamela's expression as she spoke. Rachel was aware that many birth mothers choose not to have contact with the children they gave up for adoption. Rachel hoped Pamela would not have to deal with another rejection. She reached for another book on her shelf. This one was called Lost and Found: The Adoption Experience, by Betty Jean Lifton.

"I don't know how my parents will react, either. I think my father would understand, but I bet my mother would be very angry."

"Do you plan to talk with them about your search?"

"I know I should. I just don't know how to broach the subject with them."

Maybe this will help." Rachel handed Pamela the book.

"Thanks!"

"The book interviews many adoptees about their searches and their outcomes."

"That's perfect!"

As Pamela continued discussing her interest in finding her birth mother, an idea occurred to her. She could simply tell her parents the truth. Pamela could explain that she wanted to contact Ann Kenney to tell her about her future plans. About attending college, and especially about having children someday. They would have to understand that.

Now that Pamela was completing applications for college, she realized in retrospect just how embarrassed she had become about not applying last year. It was like a cloud hanging over her identity. If she managed to get accepted, Pamela knew she would feel like her life was finally in her control. That she was adult enough to make some good decisions for herself. She wanted to share this new adult self with her birth mother, as well as with her adoptive parents.

Pamela scheduled her next appointment with Rachel, and felt motivated to talk to her parents when she arrived home.

"Mom, Dad, I have to talk to you about something," she started.

They were finishing dinner. "We're all ears," came her father's reply.

Pamela took a deep breath. "I want to write to my birth mother," Pamela muttered softly. "I just want her to know a little about me, and I'd like to know something about her, too."

Nelson Windsor was not surprised by his daughter's announcement. "I was expecting that you'd eventually want to find her," he commented. "I can show you your birth certificate if you need it. We would never stop you from searching, honey, if that's what you want. I hope you won't forget us though." Her father sighed.

"No, Daddy, of course not!" Pamela hadn't called her father 'Daddy' in many years. She looked across the table and noticed tears forming in her mother's eyes. "Are you okay, Mom?" Pamela questioned.

Her mother just shook her head, and had no verbal response to Pamela's question. She placed her napkin on the table and stood up to leave the room.

"Mom?" Pamela stood to follow her mother.

Roberta Windsor sat on an upholstered chair in her bedroom. Pamela entered behind her. The room was dark.

"Mom, are you okay?" she repeated.

"I feel like I'm losing you," her mother whispered.

"I don't want to subtract anyone from my life," Pamela responded. "I just want to add her."

Roberta Windsor looked up at her daughter. "This is more complicated than any math problem, Pammy."

Pamela had an ugly feeling inside. It was anger, she thought, salted with resentment, and peppered with some type of strange competition.

Why do I always end up taking care of you? Don't you see I have feelings? Isn't this *my* crisis?

Pamela said nothing. That evening, in the tranquil moments before sleep, Pamela once again allowed herself the fantasy of a birth mother who would know how to love her.

Chapter 7

Pamela stared at the telephone on her desk. She had asked Tracy to sit with her while she called Catholic Charities. Pamela had looked up the telephone number, procrastinated, and now her lunch hour was coming to an end. The seven digits appeared frozen on the scrap paper on her desk.

"Tracy, you dial. Hand me the phone when it rings."

Tracy followed her friend's directions. Pamela reached for the phone. She heard herself speaking but hardly recognized her own voice.

"Yes, hello, I was adopted and I think you have my birth records. I'm looking for my mother…"

"Hold on, please, our Adoption Counselor will be right with you."

Pamela was transferred to a woman who identified herself as Beth. After a brief discussion, Beth had verified the name of Pamela's birth mother and reiterated the information her father had given to her. Beth told Pamela that if she wrote a letter requesting contact, Catholic Charities would forward the letter to the last known address of Pamela's birth mother. Pamela would then have to wait for a response. Catholic Charities acted as a liaison regarding the initial contact, Beth said, as long as both parties mutually decided to continue correspondence. Some problems could arise, Beth warned. For example, the agency might not have accurate information about her birth mother's current location. Or, in the worst case scenario, her birth mother could specifically state that she wanted no contact. *Rejection*, Pamela thought, and gulped some water from the mug on her desk. Her mouth remained dry.

"I understand," she told Beth. "Would I send the letter to Catholic Charities, to your attention?"

"That would be fine. Some people like to enclose a photograph as well. And I'll need your current address and telephone number."

Pamela gave Beth the information she requested and thanked her for her assistance. She turned to Tracy, who sat silently, expectantly, her eyes wide and bright.

"What happened?"

Pamela explained the content of her discussion to her friend. "Thanks for the moral support, Tracy."

"No problem. Are you gonna write?"

"Of course! I've had whole sentences floating around in my head for years. There's a lot I want to tell her, but I'll just compose a simple letter at first. I don't want to scare her off. Her family might not know about me, Tracy. She might not want contact."

"That's true, I guess. I think most people would be curious about a child they gave up for adoption, though. Well, good luck with the letter. I'm excited for you! I'd better get back to my desk – it's one o'clock."

At home that evening, Pamela added the finishing touches to her two college essays, explaining the reasons for her dipping grades in her senior year of high school, as well as her new enthusiasm about learning. She enclosed the money orders in their respective envelopes.

Pamela put her pen down momentarily. Her heart began to race as she thought seriously about sending a letter to her birth mother. *Maybe I'm ready to contact her.* Such a mixture of feelings washed over her that each was hard to define. She thought she could isolate fear, excitement, sadness, hopefulness, anticipation and relief. Pamela closed her eyes and took a few deep breaths. Pamela picked up her pen again, and watched the words that had remained sequestered in her mind for so long appear on the page.

Dear Ann Kenney,

I have been thinking about writing to you for a long time. I have some questions only you can answer, and I would like to tell you a little about myself. I don't want to disrupt your life or complicate it in any way, but I do hope you will consider contacting me. I have enclosed a picture from my high school graduation. I will look forward to your response.

Yours truly,

Pamela Windsor

Pamela printed her home and work numbers beneath her signature. Pamela wondered if 'Yours truly' was too intense. She decided to leave the letter as it was, hoping Ann Kenney would appreciate the symbolism.

Pamela mailed all three envelopes at once, at the Springfield Post Office prior to work the next day. It was the morning that President Clinton's acquittal was anticipated. The sky looked especially blue to Pamela, and an excitement rose inside of her like none she had ever known. Pamela knew that the responses she would receive to the mail she sent today could change her life forever. And she had a good feeling about Ann Kenney.

The first response arrived quickly. Within a few days, a letter from Antioch informed Pamela that her application had been received, and an interview date had been scheduled. Pamela sent the enclosed post card back to Antioch to confirm her interview appointment with Professor Helene Chisholm. I'll have to ask Mr. Hansen for the day off, Pamela resolved. And if my father accompanies me, I can talk to him about my adoption search on the way to New Hampshire. The appointment was three weeks away, on a Thursday. That was plenty of time for Pamela's father to clear his work schedule.

"Nelson Windsor here."

"Hi, Dad, it's Pamela. Are you busy?"

"I always have time for you, sweetie."

"I heard from Antioch today, and they want to interview me on Thursday, March 11th. Do you think you could drive me there? I'm afraid I'm gonna be really nervous."

"Let me check my calendar, honey. Let's see…March 11th. Looks clear. I'll tell my secretary not to schedule any meetings for that day."

"Thanks, Dad."

"I'm glad you asked. It'll give us some time to talk. I think the drive should be under two hours. Do you have directions?"

"Antioch sent them."

"Then we're all set. Did you ask Mom to go?"

"No, I didn't."

"Do you want me to ask her?"

"I guess so." Pamela frowned. She had wanted to talk to her father alone.

"OK, sweetie, I'll see you later tonight. Gotta go."

Pamela made a mental note to talk about her mother during her next visit to Rachel. Her father seemed not to notice the awkwardness between them. He wanted to believe that his daughter and his wife had no problems at all.

* * * * * * * * * * * * * * * * *

"I have an interview for college in New Hampshire in March," Pamela told Rachel. "I asked my father to come with me. He wanted my mother to join us, but when he asked her about it, she said she was going to a Patient Support Group. The dialysis center is holding its first group meeting on the night of my interview. I'm glad she's not coming with us, because I wanted to talk to my father alone. About the adoption search."

"What's difficult about talking to your mother?"

"She's always critical. For as long as I can remember, she's been mean to me. I can't remember ever hearing her say 'I love you.' And when I try to tell her something, she doesn't seem to care about what I think."

"Give me an example."

"I hate being called Pammy. It might seem like a small thing, but I hate it. When I tell her how I feel, she just continues to call me Pammy. Like my opinions don't matter at all. I've been thinking that this kind of thing between my mother and I might explain why I thought I had no opinions. And sometimes her tone is very sarcastic. The other night, I told my parents about my interest in finding my birth mother. My mother got upset and left the dinner table. I followed her into her room and tried to ease her mind a little. It didn't help. She just made a sarcastic comment and didn't talk to me for the rest of the night."

"How did you feel about that?"

"Well, I used to feel that I had done something wrong when she acted like that. But I know it's not wrong to want to find my biological family. I felt kind of angry, in a way. It was weird."

"Can you describe your anger?"

"It was like a competitive anger. I'm not sure how to describe it." Pamela nearly apologized, but stopped herself.

"If you could give your anger a voice, what would you have said to your mother?"

"I don't know."

"You don't have to answer right away."

Pamela thought for a few moments. "Why did you adopt me if you didn't want me?" she muttered. "I know what I really wanted to say, but it might not be true. I wanted to tell her that she isn't my real mother, and that my real mother would know how to treat me! And this adoption stuff is hard for *me, too*. Why can't she be there for me? Why do I have to take care of her? She's supposed to be my mother!" Pamela began to cry. "You listen to me better than she ever did! She didn't even think I should see a counselor. She blamed me for not talking to her about things. But I *can't* talk to her! I know why I said competitive anger before. It's like I'm constantly thinking I'll prove to you that I'm worth something! But then I give up on myself. And I go nowhere. I start to think I'm not loveable."

"What's the saddest part about all this for you, Pamela?"

"That I don't feel like I've ever had a mother." Pamela paused, and sighed through her tears. "What if my birth mother doesn't want me either?"

"Are you having second thoughts about your search?"

"Not really. In the book you gave me, lots of adoptees confront parents who have no interest in knowing them. Some of them still say the search was worthwhile. No matter what happens, I still think it will help me to figure out who I am, and to know more about my heritage. In my head, I know that I'll be okay even if she has no interest in me. In my heart, though, sometimes I can still hear a little baby crying for her mother."

"Is it the 'little baby' part of you that wants to find your birth mother?"

"Mostly. But it's also my adult self, curious about my beginnings. I forgot to tell you! I wrote a letter to her! Well, to the agency, really. Just a short letter, a few lines to tell her I'm interested in contacting her. I mailed it on the same day as my college applications. I can't even look at my mailbox without getting goose bumps! I can't wait to hear something! Can I ask you something?"

"Certainly."

"If I get into school and leave Springfield, can I write to you?"

"Absolutely!" Rachel made an effort to curb her enthusiasm, as well as her New York accent. In speaking certain words, Rachel's accent was still apparent. Her colleagues teased her about the word coffee, which she still pronounced 'cawfee.'

"And when I come back here to visit, can I make an appointment to see you?"

"That would be fine."

"Pamela felt relieved. She spoke about college for the rest of her session, and scheduled an appointment for the following week. It was a cold night, and Pamela drove home listening to the radio. Bonnie Raitt was singing lyrics more chilling than the cold. *'I can't make you love me if you don't…'*

That entire refrain imprinted itself in Pamela's mind, and she was humming to herself when she entered the house. The telephone was ringing. She quickly climbed the stairs to her bedroom, and had no time to remove her winter coat before answering.

"Hello?"

"Is Pamela Windsor at home?"

"This is Pamela."

"Pamela, this is Ann Kenney…Ann Sullivan is my name now. My mother just delivered your letter to my house, and I wanted to get in touch with you as soon as possible." Pamela's heart soared. "You see, I can't have you writing to this address, or calling the house. I'm sorry."

"But I don't have any information about where you live. It's the agency that sent the letter."

"I know, but I can't have my husband seeing anything from the agency, either. He knows nothing about your existence. Please don't write again."

"Okay, but I was hoping…"

"What is it that you'd like to know?"

Is this woman for real? Pamela thought. *She's my mother; I want to know everything!* "Well, why you gave me up, and…"

"I was sixteen years old, Irish Catholic, and unmarried. The boy was older, but he wasn't interested in a commitment. I had no choice…"

"Do you have any children now?"

"I have one teenage son. His name is Paul. Is everything okay in your life? Did your family treat you well?"

"Everything's okay," Pamela sighed. "I was hoping I could meet you, to talk more about all this in person."

"I don't think that's possible. I'll think about it. *I'll* call *you*. And please, no more letters, okay?"

"I don't even know where you live."

"I'm not far from you, in Northern Connecticut."

"Maybe we could meet somewhere. I could pretend to be someone else, I don't care about that. You wouldn't have to tell your family about me."

"I could never tell them about you. My son has been complaining for a long time about being an only child. He'd never forgive me. And my husband would never understand."

"Well, I don't want to cause any problems for you…"

"You look a lot like I did at nineteen, Pamela."

"They sent you the photograph?"

"Yes, it's quite amazing, actually. You look lovely."

"Thanks." Pamela was at a loss for words. The silence grew more uncomfortable.

"I'm glad you're okay, Pamela. Take care of yourself."

"Will you call again?"

"I don't know."

Pamela replaced the telephone receiver with an unsteady hand and removed her coat. *I'm shaking like a leaf,* Pamela thought. But leaves have branches to hold on to, with trees to nurture them through life's storms. It was an inaccurate analogy, Pamela thought cynically. I'm not a leaf, I have no tree, and I'm shaking all alone.

Without thinking, Pamela picked up the receiver again. She dialed the number she knew by heart.

"Hello?"

"Hi, Brian, it's me, Pamela."

"So you finally decided to return my call?"
"I've been busy…"
"Busy with anyone I know?"
"I'm not seeing anyone, if that's what you mean."
"Why don't you come over, then? My parents aren't around tonight. I rented a video we can watch."
"Well, I…"
"Are you coming or not?"
"Okay, I'll come over."

Pamela showered and changed her clothes. She was tired, and had second thoughts about her plans to see Brian again. *Maybe he'll distract me from that hellish phone call,* she thought. Choking back tears, determined to be strong, Pamela walked the few blocks to Brian's house.

"Hey, come on in. You must be cold."

Pamela took a long time to remove her coat. The video was already in the VCR, and Pamela realized quickly that Brian was watching another horror movie. Brian would constantly tease Pamela whenever the films frightened her. He enjoyed them, and seemed to find it amusing when Pamela became startled by them.

Tonight, though, she was hardly paying attention. Brian had asked her if she wanted a glass of soda, and she had said yes. She hardly noticed when he sat down next to her on the couch, and put his arm around her. When his other arm began stroking her leg, Pamela became startled. Brian laughed, assuming she had been affected in her usual way be the movie. His hand traveled to her cardigan, and he began undoing the buttons. He reached around to the middle of her back and undid her bra as well. Pamela sat motionless on the couch, staring straight ahead. Her life was a horror film. He pulled at her breasts and sucked on her nipples, holding one and then the other, breathing hard. He smelled like petroleum. His nails had dirt underneath them. Pamela tried to pull away.

"Don't get frigid on me, Pamela. You called *me*, remember?"

"I can't do this." Pamela barely heard her own voice.

"Don't worry, I won't get you pregnant again."

Brian unzipped his jeans, and reached for Pamela's hand. She resisted. He pulled her arm by the wrist, and forced her hand underneath the elastic band of his underwear. She could not avoid his penis.

"Feel how hard you've made me," he said. "Don't tease me like this."

A woman screamed in the horror film. Once Brian realized that Pamela planned to keep her hand still, he removed it and stood in front of her. Pamela remained seated. She had no energy to fight. Brian was much stronger than she was. Pamela felt defeated and alone. She stared at her bra on the carpet in front of her. One button of her cardigan remained buttoned around her waist, and her bare breasts were exposed. While her head was down, Brian grabbed her by the hair. She opened her mouth with a grimace, and Brian shoved his penis into it. He held her seated on the couch with one arm on her shoulder. He was hurting her now. Pamela tried to protect the back of her throat with her tongue as Brian continued to thrust himself into her. She soon tasted his warm, sour ejaculation and knew her ordeal was ending. Brian collected himself and released his grip. Pamela rose from the couch. She buttoned her cardigan, picked up her bra and folded it neatly. She reached for her coat, and placed the bra in her coat pocket. She was in a daze.

"What's wrong with you, anyway? Where do you think you're going?"

Brian's tone was angry. Pamela watched him shake his head at her in disgust. She left his house without uttering a word.

Pamela arrived home and quietly climbed the stairs. She filled the bathtub with hot water and soaked her sore muscles. Her neck and shoulder ached. She couldn't recall Brian being so forceful with her in the past. After a long bath, she retired to her room and thought about calling Rachel. Rachel had told Pamela that she could call the answering service at Access Health Center at any time, and that they would contact Rachel in an emergency. Was this an emergency? Pamela thought not. She was embarrassed. She had caused her own misery. And it scared

Pamela a little bit to be thinking about calling Rachel. Pamela was afraid that she was getting too dependent on Rachel. She reasoned that Rachel was nurturing toward her, like a mother should be. She felt that Rachel understood her, and was genuinely interested in her. She wondered if Rachel actually liked her, or if she was just doing her job. She knew so little about Rachel. It was hard for Pamela to have asked Rachel those questions about sending letters and keeping in touch. But she didn't want to abruptly end the relationship if she moved away. Something was scary about Rachel being like a mother to Pamela. 'Mother' had such negative connotations. Pamela didn't want to leave the area and be forced to leave the only person who acted like a mother toward her. How many mothers would she have to lose in one lifetime?

Pamela managed to sleep soundly and awoke early. She called in sick to work. She ate and slept excessively for the next few days, licking her emotional wounds. Tracy called to see how she was feeling. Pamela lied and told her friend she had the flu. She tried to focus on some neglected chores around the house. On Friday morning, she took the garbage pail to the street, and collected the mail. *A letter from the University of Colorado!* Pamela ran inside and grabbed the letter opener on the kitchen counter. She opened the letter neatly, just in case she wanted to save its contents for posterity. An acceptance to school would mean so much right now…

The letter said that although Pamela's credentials were impressive, the school had received an abundance of applications for the coming academic year, and they could not accept her into the fall class. The letter suggested that she reapply in the coming year, and wished her luck in her academic pursuits.

Pamela stared blankly at the signature on the letter. That was it. It was all too much. Her birth mother's rejection for the *second* time, Brian, and now this. Pamela had some insight in that moment as to why she was so upset about Brian breaking up with her on her birthday. It was kind of an ironic reminder of the original rejection by Ann Kenney

Sullivan. Pamela burst into bitter tears, pitying herself. She thought of Rachel's encouragement, empowering her toward success. Rachel had been wasting her time on Pamela. It was no use. Pamela was destined to fail, to keep being dismissed throughout her life. Pamela tore up the rejection letter, and called Access Health Center. She cancelled her appointment with Rachel for the following Monday.

"Do you want her to call you back to reschedule?" asked the receptionist politely.

"No, just tell her I have to work late, and *I'll* call *her*."

Chapter 8

"As usual, Rachel, your outpatient treatment reports are excellent. You support your diagnoses well. I wanted to review one case at length with you today. Are you still counseling Pamela Windsor?"

Rachel stiffened. "I think so," she nodded. Pamela had not called to reschedule her appointment. It had been several weeks. Rachel's supervisor, Dr. Ed Weiser, was a licensed psychologist who had tremendous insight and a great talent for working with people, especially children. He dressed casually and had a kind face with warm, penetrating eyes. Ed Weiser did things by the book.

"I don't see any casenotes for the past few weeks. Have you spoken with her?"

"No, I haven't. Her message specifically stated that she would call to reschedule. Do you think I should call her?"

"No, there would be no way to assess her level of motivation to continue treatment if you called her."

"But maybe she's waiting to hear from me, waiting for me to reach out to her. Pamela doesn't feel very cared about in her life."

"Is this the adopted young woman you've spoken about, whose presenting problem was having had an abortion?"

Rachel was consistently impressed by her supervisor's memory for detail. Rachel saw more than 25 clients, and Dr. Weiser supervised five other therapists. "Yes, that's Pamela."

"Tell me what you think is going on."

"Pamela has been extremely reliable about keeping her appointments. This is her first cancellation. In our last session, she asked me about the possibility of keeping in touch if she decides to relocate to attend college this fall. I know she values her treatment, but she fears rejection from people. She had just written to her birth mother and sent applications to colleges. I'm wondering if she received negative responses and is having trouble facing me as a result. Maybe she thinks I'll be disappointed or angry."

"So you think this is about negative transference."

"Somewhat. But I also think I represent hope, guidance, maybe even a 'good mother' to her. And if Pamela's been rejected, she may be feeling undeserving of those things."

"My dilemma is this, Rachel. This is a busy clinic, as you know, and our policy is to close cases after three weeks without client contact. We have a form letter we use, stating that we haven't heard from her in several weeks…"

"I can't send a form letter. It doesn't feel right. I'm not ready to close the case." Rachel had never challenged Ed Weiser before. She felt herself becoming emotional, and did not want to lose her professional edge.

"*You're* not ready, but Pamela might be. She may have already gotten what she needed from you. Do you have some countertransference issues we need to address?"

"Well, I do feel a different kind of connection with Pamela…"

"Is she triggering something from your own history? I'm not your therapist, but is there something you'd like to tell me that will clarify your clinical relationship?"

"I had an abortion as a teenager also," Rachel blurted out. "My mother had recently died, and I waited a long time before I told anyone I was pregnant. I had a second-trimester abortion because my father insisted upon it. I wanted to have the baby. I even fantasized that my mother's spirit would somehow inhabit the baby…I hoped it would be a little girl. I've been talking about this in my own therapy…"

"How long ago did you have the abortion, Rachel?"

"Nineteen years ago in June."

"And how old is Pamela?"

Rachel confirmed Pamela's birth date by checking her face sheet data. "She's…nineteen." A sadness enveloped Rachel, and nearly overcame her.

"So you have a positive countertransference to Pamela. She's the age your unborn child would have been. And you're the mother to whom she finally feels connected. That creates an interesting dynamic. I can certainly understand that Pamela's treatment would take on a special significance for you, but I can only keep the case open for another week. If she doesn't call you by then, you'll have to send the letter. I have other referrals for you. Sometimes termination of a case entails loss for the therapist, too."

Rachel resisted referring to Pamela as a 'case', but she nodded her agreement to Dr. Weiser. He briefly reviewed her work with several other clients, noting that she continued to have successful short-term treatment outcomes. They scheduled a meeting in two weeks. Rachel collected her files and briefcase, said goodnight to Hilary at the front desk, and was glad to be returning home for the evening.

Glen had left the outside light on for Rachel. She discovered a note inside the condo that said he'd be out with some friends from work. "I'll probably be late, don't wait up. All my love, Glen." Rachel read aloud. She trusted her husband implicitly. Rachel often counseled women in relationships to cope with their suspicions and distrust of their partners. Often, they felt abandoned by their husbands. Glen took his marriage vows very seriously. He was devoted to her. Rachel was very lucky and she knew it.

In the kitchen, Rachel found another note. Glen's firm had catered lunch at work, it said. His fellow supervisor was leaving, and Glen had rescued some of the catered food for Rachel's dinner. The leftovers awaited her in the refrigerator.

A post-it was attached to the plastic wrap on the dish of food. Glen had written 'I adore you' across the post-it in his neat handwriting. "I adore you, too." Rachel said aloud. She heated the tofu and broccoli that Glen had carefully placed over brown rice. She noticed that a videotape recording labeled 'Dateline' was sitting on the coffee table. Rachel surmised that Glen must have taped it, and decided to watch it.

Rachel was glad she had finished eating by the time Juanita Broderick's story aired. The woman accused the President of having coerced her sexually. She described being raped in her own hotel room twenty years ago. The description contained vivid detail, and she exhibited acute upset about the incident. Rachel thought the woman seemed believable. In a few moments, Rachel began a battle with herself to remove her father's face from her mind. She smelled the alcohol on his breath. She could feel his groping hands. It had been nineteen years, but Rachel still suffered from occasional symptoms of post-traumatic stress. The aftereffects of her abuse had decreased in severity, frequency and duration. Rachel seldom experienced the pain and terror that had haunted her early years in incest therapy, and which were always present in her initial flashbacks. But a story like Juanita Broderick's could still provoke some intrusive memory in Rachel.

Rachel continued to cope with intrusive images of her father, and intrusive thoughts. She battered herself about her abortion. After the operation, she had confronted her father, and the abuse had stopped. She had taken control. Why hadn't she confronted him earlier? Why didn't she fight back? Rachel knew intellectually that the abuse was not her fault and that she had perceived her father to be dangerous, but she still struggled emotionally. She had read numerous books like The Courage to Heal, about surviving sexual abuse. Rachel knew she had no 'bad core'. But there was still a thirteen-year-old girl living inside her who refused to believe that sometimes.

The saddest part for Rachel was that she could not allow herself to feel sexual pleasure. It was as if her father had kidnapped her ability to enjoy sex, and he continued to hold it hostage. Somehow, there was also a profound connection between her guilt about her abortion and her guilt about enjoying sex. Glen seemed to realize that Rachel could not bring herself to discuss her intimacy problems with him. Glen had good boundaries, and would always respect her need for emotional privacy. Someday, she thought, I'll be ready to conquer that last obstacle. I want to enjoy sex fully with Glen.

Rachel knew that sometimes bereaved mothers whose children had died avoided sexual intimacy. Sometimes grief produced so much guilt that people avoided experiencing any pleasure at all. This sexual stuff was like that for Rachel. Some incest survivors felt sexual pleasure during their abuse. They coped with many confusing aftereffects as adults. Rachel only remembered pain. Other survivors had no memory of love from either parent. Rachel felt fortunate to have had such a loving mother until she was eleven years old.

The ringing of the telephone jarred Rachel from her thoughts.

"Hello?"

"Hi, Rachel, it's Aunt Lynn. How are you?"

"Good! What about you?"

"I'm just fine. The girls are coming home with the grandkids in a few weeks, I know they'd love to see you. Easter Sunday falls on the first Sunday in April this year. Do you think you and Glen could come to Amherst for an early dinner?"

"We'd love to!"

"Good, honey, how's everything?"

"Well, work is busy. Glen and I are good…"

"Things are good here too. I'm still baking up a storm. The grandkids miss their grandmother's home cooking, you know."

"Of course they do. We look forward to your cooking too, Aunt Lynn."

"Terrific. It's late, I'll let you go. See you soon! How does one o'clock sound?"

"We'll be there."

Aunt Lynn had been like a second mother to Rachel. She remembered the long distance phone call to Aunt Lynn that had changed her life. Rachel had returned to Neil's house after her abortion, and had opened the address book she had taken from her mother's bureau. Rachel prayed that the book would hold some answers for her. On it's first page, her Aunt Lynn's name and address jumped out at her. Lynn Andrews was written in capital letters. Her street address followed, and finally, Amherst, Massachusetts. The 413 area code was written in black ink, and the telephone number was in red. Rachel requested permission from Mrs. Stark, Neil's mother, to call the number collect. Her aunt must have received a large phone bill that month, because their conversation lasted for nearly an hour. Finally, her Aunt Lynn had made sense of the chaos that Rachel never understood.

"Aunt Lynn?"

"Who is this?"

"It's Rachel, Janine's daughter."

"Well, hello there, Rachel. How is your mother?"

Oh, my God, she doesn't know. My stupid father never told them. That's why they never came to the funeral. But why didn't my mother tell her own sister about the cancer?"

"She had cancer, Aunt Lynn. She died almost two years ago."

"Oh, my God! How awful! Why didn't she tell me? Oh, honey, I'm so sorry. You mother loved you very much. You must miss her terribly." Rachel could hear that her aunt was crying. "Are you...oh, my God!...are you living with your father?"

"Yes, but I..."

"Is he hurting you?"

"...Yes," Rachel confessed.

"That bastard! He used to hit your mother all the time. They fought before she married him. Your mother was a stubborn woman, Rachel, she wouldn't listen to her family. We knew he had a drinking problem, and it seemed like every time he had a few beers too many she'd end up with a black eye, or bruises on her arms. One time he dislocated her shoulder. Did she tell you about that, Rachel?"

"No…"

"Well, I think you should know. She'd tell us she was leaving him and we'd take her in, your grandmother Ruth and me. We'd keep her here and dress her wounds and then in a few weeks, he'd start looking for her again. We helped her in every way we knew how, honey, but she always went back to him. And then he proposed, and she married him. She became pregnant with you on her honeymoon. He even hit her while she was pregnant; can you believe that? He'd apologize and act real remorseful afterwards until it happened again. But after you were born, she told us she couldn't leave him. Ever. We saw you for a few years; do you remember honey? The summers you spent here? But your grandmother Ruth and I just got tired of talking to her about divorce. I'll never understand it. We did the wrong thing, honey. We disowned your mother. I just couldn't stand to see her hurt anymore. We made her choose between her husband and her family. Oh, my God, we should've stuck by her! Now look what's happened!" Aunt Lynn was sobbing. "You can't stay there, honey. You're taking the train to Springfield and moving in with me, do you hear? I'll deal with your father about it. I have two extra rooms here. Both my daughters are away at college. Do you remember Margaret and Sarah?"

"Yes, a little. But I have school for another few weeks. I'm staying with a friend and his family."

"Give me your phone number." Rachel knew Neil's number by heart. "This is what you'll do. You start to collect some boxes from the supermarket. You pack the things you want to take in those boxes. You wrap your clothes around the breakables. I'll send you some money so you can mail the boxes to me in Amherst. Then you call Amtrak and you get yourself a one-way ticket to Springfield, Massachusetts. I'll pay for that, too. Can you get yourself to Penn Station?"

"Yes."

"Do you know where the big ticket counter is, upstairs from the Long Island Railroad?"

"I think so."

"Good girl. You let me know your arrival date and time and I'll be at the train station waiting for you. How old are you now, Rachel?"

"I'm 13."

"My goodness. How did you manage to find me?"

"You're on the first page of my mother's old address book. And thank you, Aunt Lynn, I'm so happy I called. Thank you for everything."

"Don't mention it, honey. You're family. I won't make that mistake again. Now put your friend's mother on the phone, so I can thank her for doing my job for me!"

Neil accompanied Rachel to Manhattan, and carried her bags. She gave him her Aunt Lynn's address and telephone number, and he promised to write. When Rachel arrived in Springfield, her Aunt Lynn was there to greet her as promised. She searched her aunt's face for some resemblance to her mother as they drove to Amherst together. When they reached their destination, Aunt Lynn showed Rachel Emily Dickinson's home, which was now a museum. They drove along the quaint Main Street. It was lovely, but so different from Long Island. Rachel felt as if she were being rescued by her aunt. She hoped she would be able to adjust to her new surroundings. Rachel would have the entire summer to think about that. Her aunt drove Rachel to the beautiful Victorian home she remembered from summers long ago. There were flowers all along the wraparound porch, and she remembered sitting in the porch swing with her mother. Rachel was noticeably withdrawn as she entered the house with her aunt.

"Are you okay, Rachel?"

"I'm happy and sad at the same time, Aunt Lynn. This house brings back wonderful memories. I'm so glad to be here, but I don't have my Mom with me anymore."

"I'm happy and sad too, honey. Your Mom's photographs are all over this house. I'm so glad you're here, and I miss your mother, too. I bet she'd be glad you're here. We'll have to do the best we can without her, okay?"

Grandma Ruth lived upstairs in that house. Aunt Lynn took care of her. She had bad arthritis and needed help with things. Grandma Ruth hugged Rachel with tears in her eyes.

"You look like my Janine," she said. Grandma Ruth brought Rachel to her mother's old room. "We cleared the closet and drawers out for you, honey. We thought it might be nice for you to be around some of your mother's old things. That's her old bureau, and her photographs are hanging over there."

Rachel looked around. It was peaceful to be close to her mother in this way. "Thank you," she told them both. "I'll start to unpack my boxes."

Lynn Andrews noticed Rachel's necklace for the first time. "That looks familiar…"

"It's the one you bought for Mom. It was her favorite."

Lynn Andrews hugged her niece, and left the room in tears.

Rachel remembered hearing her father's voice later that evening, yelling into the telephone at Aunt Lynn. "You'll raise her to be a dyke like you!" His slurred speech was apparent, and Rachel was glad that her Aunt Lynn had hung up the telephone without allowing him to continue. Rachel was frightened that her father would force her to return to Long Island. Aunt Lynn assured her that he would not. She could prove he was violent, Aunt Lynn had said. And it was obvious that he had a drinking problem. He couldn't take care of her properly. Aunt Lynn asked Rachel to join her at the kitchen table.

"Rachel, do you remember me saying that we disowned your Mom?"

"Yes..."

"Well, there was more to it than that. After my divorce, I told the family I was gay. Your mother had some trouble with the idea, but it was your father who couldn't accept me. I think your father forbade your mother to have contact with me; he thinks homosexuality is a sin."

Homosexuality! Rachel thought. *How about rape?!* "My father shouldn't be judging other people."

"I agree with you, honey. But some people are frightened by things they don't understand. Now, mind you, I'm not in a relationship right now, but many of my friends are gay, and from time to time, you'll be meeting some of them..."

"That's fine with me," Rachel remarked, and she meant it.

"Good. Margaret and Sarah had no problems accepting me, either, like you. They have a 'live and let live' attitude about people. But now you understand why your mother stopped visiting. It wasn't just her marriage that was the problem."

"My father was the problem. Sometimes I wonder if my mother chose to die to escape from her life with him."

"Your Mom loved you too much to choose to die, honey. But I hope she's in a better place now."

"Me, too, Aunt Lynn. I hope she knows we're a family again."

It had been a long time since Rachel had thought about the telephone call her father had made to Aunt Lynn. Aunt Lynn had always been discreet about her relationships, and her sexual preferences never bothered Rachel. Aunt Lynn's two daughters, Margaret and Sarah, were both happily married and maintained good relationships with both of their parents. And if anyone had the potential to turn Rachel off to men, it was her own father, Brendon Abbott, not her wonderful Aunt Lynn.

Rachel had spent her high school years in the library, concentrating on maintaining her status in the National Honor Society. She dated a few young men, but did not attend her senior prom. Rachel remained mistrustful of relationships. Most young men didn't seem to notice her, anyway. Rachel had been plain-looking as a teenager. She was lanky and androgynous, with fine long brown hair that hung around her face, and deep brown eyes. Rachel did not exaggerate her femininity in the ways that some of the other girls did. She wore no make-up or nail polish. Her tortoise-shell glasses adorned her face, and Rachel's only piece of jewelry was her mother's necklace. Rachel was most comfortable in baggy clothing that hid her body. In form-fitting clothing, Rachel felt exposed and transparent. Rachel later discovered in therapy that her clothing expressed her desire to be invisible, to focus on *not* being noticed. The abused child inside Rachel believed that she could avoid more abuse if she remained 'invisible'. Instead, Rachel learned as an adult that she could make other choices to protect herself, and to redefine safety. It was wonderful not to perceive herself as a victim any longer.

When Rachel began to attend college classes at the University of Massachusetts at Amherst, her Aunt Lynn was instrumental in convincing her to trade her glasses in for contact lenses. She also began wearing her hair differently, and her aunt bought her some stylish clothing. It was at the University of Massachusetts that a few men noticed her. One of them was Glen Moss. Glen and Rachel were enrolled in the same Sociology class, and Glen reminded Rachel of her old friend Neil on Long Island. He was smart and friendly, much more outgoing and sociable than Rachel. He seemed enthusiastic about their conversations, and soon they were sharing their values, hopes and dreams. Rachel realized that she had been very lonely for someone like Glen. She had no regrets about becoming more involved with him, and he gradually helped her to trust men again. Glen awakened Rachel's sexuality, and although that frightened her, she was ready to explore that part of herself. He was patient and understanding when she grew uncomfortable sexually, and seemed to value other parts of their relationship just as highly as their intimate contact. They were companions who enjoyed each others company immensely, and they respected each others differences. When Glen proposed marriage, Rachel was ready to make that commitment to him. She thought it was a bit corny, but Glen personified the idea of *soulmate* to Rachel. She had no doubts about their compatibility. They had come a long way together.

Rachel decided to follow Glen's advice and retire to bed. She would not wait up for him tonight. She cleared her mind of the bad memories that had resurfaced, and enjoyed the sounds of the ocean on the relaxation tape she had played before succumbing to sleep.

Chapter 9

If Pamela hadn't asked her father to accompany her to her interview at Antioch, she knew she would have cancelled it. Now he was waiting downstairs for her, expecting her to be all nervous and jittery about it. Pamela was not nervous at all. She had given up all hope of becoming a college student. She dressed in one of her comfortable knit dresses from work, and slipped into a pair of leather boots. She threw a blazer over her shoulders. Her hair had not responded well to her blow-drying efforts this morning, but she didn't care. What did it matter, anyway?

Pamela sat down in front of a plate of scrambled eggs and toast which her father had lovingly prepared for her. "A good breakfast will help you think more clearly at your interview," he told her. She smiled and tried to feign interest. This would be a long trip, Pamela thought.

"Pamela, you said you wanted to talk to me," her father began once they had made their way to Route 91 North. "Did you decide to go ahead with your plans to search for your birth mother? You haven't mentioned anything to me, and you seem very quiet. Is everything okay?"

Pamela tried not to cry, to preserve her mascara. "Not really, Dad. I wrote a letter to her. She called me, but only to tell me that she wanted nothing to do with me."

"Honey, that's awful! How long ago did she call you?"

"A few weeks ago."

"I'm sorry, Pamela. Tell me about the conversation."

Pamela found herself grateful for her father's interest. She discussed what she remembered from her short conversation with Ann Kenney Sullivan. As Pamela spoke, she discovered that she was simultaneously gaining some perspective about the information that her birth mother had shared. Pamela began compiling the information in her mind. Pamela had discovered that she had a half-brother named Paul. Her birth mother was married and living in Northern Connecticut. Her maternal grandmother was alive, and probably still lived in the same home where her birth mother grew up. Her half-brother always wanted another sibling. Pamela resembled her birth mother in appearance. Pamela's mental wheels were turning quickly. Maybe she could still find her birth mother. Maybe she could see her half-brother Paul. Pamela decided to search the Connecticut telephone directory that her father kept in his study. There would probably be dozens of Sullivans, she thought, dismayed. Unless...*maybe Paul was named after his father!* She would search for them, beginning with the Paul Sullivans. Maybe Tracy would come to Connecticut with her. Pamela decided to call her friend after returning from New Hampshire. Pamela felt excited about something for the first time in weeks. She was still daydreaming when they arrived in Keene, New Hampshire.

Nelson Windsor had no trouble finding the Antioch campus. They had arrived a bit early, and Pamela was not quite ready to enter the building. She was nervous now. Her father had the calming influence she originally hoped he would. He spoke to her in his gentle way, and soon helped her to feel more confident about the interview. She stepped out of his car, straightened her dress, and walked into the building alone. She glanced back to wave to her father, but he was already absorbed in the newspaper. Pamela's father read the Springfield Republican daily.

The building had been renovated on the inside. It was very contemporary and welcoming. There were wide hallways and skylights everywhere.

There were signs directing newcomers to the admissions office, professors' offices and the group interview room. Pamela followed signs to the group interview room, and was greeted at the doorway by Professor Helene Chisholm. The professor was a pretty, petite woman, with dark wavy hair. She led Pamela to a circle of chairs. Pamela was the first to arrive. She busied herself by reading the pamphlets left on the chairs for each applicant. To her surprise, Pamela was able to rekindle some of her enthusiasm about Antioch. The booklets held information about the first semester's curriculum, and Pamela read further with sincere interest. As other applicants entered, Pamela noticed that they seemed nervous as well. Professor Chisholm began by discussing the requirements for the first year program, and a question-and-answer period followed. Introductions were next, and Pamela found that many of these young people had already volunteered or worked in environmental agencies. She was embarrassed to share her lack of experience, but managed to express her enthusiasm about the opportunities in the field. Professor Chisholm thanked her for her participation.

Within the hour, the group ended and Professor Chisholm asked Pamela to accompany her to her office. "You're the first person on my list of interviewees," she stated. Professor Chisholm was dressed very comfortably in a paisley broomstick skirt and sweater, with a scarf to match the skirt, and beads around her neck. She wore long, hanging silver earrings that swayed when she walked. When they arrived at her office, Professor Chisholm sat behind her desk and offered Pamela the only other chair in the room. Across from Pamela stood Professor Chisholm's bookshelves, which were filled with books. *Like Rachel's office*, Pamela thought. I have to return her books to her, Pamela remembered. I have to call her. I want to go back to counseling.

The interview went well. For twenty minutes, Pamela described her interests and minimal work experience, and answered Professor Chisholm's questions as best as she could. Professor Chisholm told Pamela that the Admissions Committee had been impressed with her personal essay. They would be making their decisions about the applicants within the next two weeks. Professor Chisholm shook Pamela's hand and thanked her for coming.

Her father was still reading the newspaper when Pamela reentered his car. Nelson Windsor looked up at his daughter. "How did it go?"

"It went okay, I think."

"Are you hungry?"

"Starving."

"Good. I took a ride earlier and found a restaurant that looked appealing."

Lunch and the ride home were pleasant. Pamela was daydreaming a lot as the sun warmed her hands on her lap inside the car. "Thanks for taking me," she remembered to say to her father.

"My pleasure, Pamela. I hope you hear from them soon."

They arrived in West Springfield, and Pamela ran upstairs to her bedroom. First, she called and rescheduled an appointment with Rachel Abbott-Moss for the following evening. The receptionist transferred the call to Rachel, who was still at work. Rachel sounded glad to hear from her, and offered Pamela a six o'clock appointment. "See you then," she told Rachel. Pamela called Tracy next. "Hold on a second!" Pamela ran downstairs and quickly found the Northern Connecticut telephone directory. She returned to a bewildered Tracy, and told the story of her birth mother's call for the second time that day. As she spoke, Pamela flipped through the white pages until the name Sullivan appeared. Her finger floated down the page until she discovered two listings of Paul Sullivan. There was another listing for a 'P. Sullivan', but Pamela thought that listing would most likely be a woman's. Two listings – both in the Enfield area! I'll start with those, Pamela decided. Tracy said she'd love to explore this with Pamela. 'A real adventure', she had called it. They made plans to travel to Enfield on Saturday morning.

* * * * * * * * * * * * * * * * *

Rachel was anxious about her session with Pamela. She had no idea what to expect. Rachel remembered the advice of her supervisor regarding transitional treatment situations. He had told her to discuss 'process as well as content'. 'Process,' Rachel knew, referred to the dynamic between the therapist and the client. 'Don't be afraid to broach the subject of your relationship,' he had said. Tonight, Rachel would try to introduce the concept of 'process' to Pamela.

"Hi. I brought your books back – thanks!" Pamela began. "I had that interview yesterday at Antioch…it went pretty well."

Is she returning the books because she's ready to leave treatment? Rachel wondered. "I'm glad it went well. I wanted to talk with you tonight about your sessions here, Pamela. I know you haven't been here in several weeks, and I wondered how you've been feeling about counseling. Do you feel like you're getting what you need here?"

"Definitely! I just had a rough couple of weeks…"

"I thought you might have. I know we spoke about crisis calls, do you remember?"

"I thought about calling you, but I changed my mind."

"Do you know why?"

"I didn't want to bother you."

"You wouldn't have. Any other reasons?"

"I didn't know if you really cared. I know I pay you to help me and everything, but I don't know anything about you. I don't know if you're just doing your job, or if you really care about me. I don't even know if I'm allowed to ask you questions."

"Sounds like you're troubled by our relationship."

"I want to trust you. I just don't know if I can. I don't think I trust anybody. I guess I'm afraid of rejection with you, too. But you've really helped me. I mean, I've been feeling better about myself."

"Is there anything I can do to help you to trust me?"

"Not reject me."

"Do you feel rejected by me?"'

"No. But you treat me like I want my mother and my birth mother to treat me. You listen to me. I guess I don't think I deserve it. I think eventually you'll reject me, too."

"Your birth mother never knew you, Pamela. She may have had reasons for not being able to keep you with her, and she may be unable to incorporate you into her life now."

"She called to tell me not to contact her again."

"I thought she might have. But her reaction may have nothing at all to do with you. And you've talked about your mother being preoccupied with her illness. They both have their own personal reasons for distancing from you. Yet you seem to blame yourself totally."

"I never looked at it that way."

"Are there other people in your life that haven't rejected you?"

"My father…my friend Tracy…and you, so far!"

"Would you say we know you well?"

"Yes."

"So your theory doesn't hold up. The opposite of what you believe is actually true. The people who know you best don't reject you."

"I wish I could stop worrying about rejection from everyone."

"Do you think there might be something good about worrying about rejection?"

"How could there be?"

"Sometimes it's hard to change a belief we have because it feels safe, or familiar…"

"I get it. I think I get it. I don't have to take any risks if I'm always fearing rejection. I can stay safe and blame myself and never challenge myself at all. I can just keep telling myself 'Why bother?' Just like I have been for the past few weeks. I guess self-pity is like quicksand for me. I fall into it and need help to get out. Do you think I might actually believe someday that I don't deserve to be rejected? It would be like really liking myself!"

"I think you're learning to like yourself right now, Pamela. And I have an assignment for you. I want you to make a list of the things that you do like about yourself, keep the list with you, and keep adding to it."

"Yuck!"

"We can talk about the difficulties you have with making the list also."

"And I guess you won't reject me if I don't do my assignment?"

"Right. But give it a try, okay?"

"Okay."

Pamela proceeded to tell Rachel about the telephone call from Ann Kenney Sullivan, the evening she had spent at Brian's house, and the rejection letter from Colorado. Pamela left out certain details about Brian's behavior, because she still wasn't sure if she trusted Rachel that much. She understood that she had withdrawn instead of reaching out, and realized that her mood had changed once she started opening up to her father. She would try to make a concerted effort to change her pattern of withdrawal. Pamela was very glad that she had returned to see Rachel.

* * * * * * * * * * * * * * * * * *

On Saturday, Tracy drove Pamela to Enfield. The two young women were equipped with two addresses. They had no map of Enfield, and planned to utilize the memories of gas station attendants to find their destinations. If all else failed, Tracy knew a great department store in Enfield where they could browse.

The first address was 121 Cedar Street. After several attempts to locate Cedar Street, they asked a jogger along the road if they were headed in the right direction. "It's the next left," he said. *Oh, my God,* Pamela thought, *this might be it.* The street was long, and Tracy spotted the number 121 on a mailbox. Tracy pulled her Toyota to the side of the road. The house was a small cottage, set back from the road, with a fenced yard and a swing set. The swing set was equipped with a slide and monkey bars. A child's pink tricycle stood in the driveway. This can't be the place, Pamela told herself. Tracy echoed her thoughts.

"You said you had a teenage brother, right? No little kids?"

"I don't think this is it, Tracy."

"Let's go to the next address."

Tracy found another gas station on the main road, and asked the attendant about 56 Sparrow Hill Lane. "Try the 'bird section,'" he announced.

"Where's that?"

"Take this road to the new development. It's called Anderson Acres. Make a right, and ask someone in that development. They should be able to help you."

Tracy located Anderson Acres. A bicyclist pulled up beside them at a stop sign.

"Is this the way to the 'bird section'?" Pamela asked.

"I don't know. Sorry."

The women drove around in the area of the new development. They decided to take each of the roads that led out of the development, and drove for miles before Tracy yelled "Robin Court!" They had found their destination.

Pamela and Tracy passed Bluebird Lane and Cardinal Drive on their left. Sparrow Hill Lane was next. "Sparrow Hill!" Tracy shouted. They found 56 Sparrow Hill Lane. The house was large and neatly landscaped. Tracy pulled the car to the side of the road. The house stood on a corner property. Tracy was able to position the car so that the front door of the house was visible. Both women were nervous. Tracy had actually packed tuna fish sandwiches and potato chips for the trip, and offered a sandwich to Pamela.

"Have some lunch, it might be a long wait."

Pamela accepted, and was thankful for the distraction. They ate in silence, watching the closed white door.

Two cars were in the driveway of 56 Sparrow Hill Lane. After lunch, Pamela and Tracy talked about college, guys, shopping and work. Everything but adoption. Tracy was more loquacious than Pamela, and they sat for hours, unnoticed, in front of the house. Just before three o'clock, Tracy observed movement at the front door.

"Pamela, I think someone is coming outside!"

Pamela's initial reaction was to duck down in her seat. "Watch for me, Tracy, I don't want to be seen."

"Oh, my goodness, Pamela, she looks just like you! She even walks like you! She's walking out to the driveway. She has a cell phone. She's talking on it. This has to be the right place.

Pamela raised her torso up slightly so that her eyes could barely see over the dashboard. At that moment, her half-brother, Paul, stepped out onto the lawn. He examined the azaleas. He had dark hair, but his features were similar to hers. Pamela's birth mother called to Paul from the driver's side of the car. Tracy had left the car windows slightly ajar.

"Let's go, Paul, we have to be back by six o'clock."

They both heard his name. "*It's them!*" Tracy whispered.

Pamela was mesmerized by her birth mother's face. It was like looking into a mirror of the future. She was petite and attractive, dressed in a cashmere coat and brown leather boots. Paul entered the passenger side of the car, and Pamela's birth mother continued her conversation on the cell phone. Ann Kenney Sullivan turned the key in the ignition of her silver Ford Taurus, and backed the car out of the driveway. She drove like she was in a very big hurry.

"Oh, my goodness, Pamela, did you see that? She just went right through that stop sign!"

"With my *brother* in the car!" Pamela exclaimed.

Although she had barely set eyes on him, Pamela felt an enormous connection to Paul Sullivan. Maybe it was the fact that she knew he never wanted to be an only child. Seeing him in the flesh and knowing that she couldn't reach out to him was devastating for Pamela. She wanted to scream, *you have a sister!* Pamela felt protective of him as well. He looked old enough to be driving. Why didn't her birth mother let him drive? He probably notices things like stop signs when he drives, she thought.

Pamela's eyes stayed fixed on the Ford Taurus until it was no longer visible. Pamela had learned something about her birth mother that she didn't care to know. Ann Kenney Sullivan appeared to be a reckless driver.

* * * * * * * * * * * * * * * * *

On Wednesday afternoon, Pamela's mother called her at work.

"Pammy, there's a big envelope here for you from Antioch. Do you want me to open it?"

Pamela cringed at hearing the name 'Pammy', but tried to control her irritation. A big envelope might be a good sign, Pamela guessed. The rejection letter from Colorado was just one page, folded in three parts, delivering the bad news. Maybe bigger meant better news. Why not? Pamela thought.

"Okay, go ahead and open it."

Pamela focused only on her mother's first words. "Congratulations, you have been accepted…" I'm in! I made it! I can't believe it! Thank you, Professor Chisholm! Pamela's mind raced. She promised herself that she would review her personal essay to figure out what was impressive about it. *They want me!*

"Pammy, are you still there?"

"I'm here, I'm just in shock!"

"Well, there are a lot of important papers in here that you'll have to look through later. Looks like some financial aid information, class description, a schedule…"

"Okay, thanks, Mom. Can you put it in my room?"

"Sure."

"Are you gonna call Dad?"

"I will if you want me to. Unless you want to tell him yourself."

"No, you tell him. I want to tell Tracy. I gotta go!"

Roberta Windsor had rarely heard so much enthusiasm in her daughter's voice. She called her husband to share the news, and spent a good part of the afternoon thinking about distance. The distance between Massachusetts and New Hampshire, the distance between health and illness, and the distance between adoptive mothers and their daughters.

Chapter 10

Mrs. Roberta Windsor was thrilled that her daughter was accepted to college, but the news was a mixed blessing. Roberta depended on her daughter, and was hopeful about sitting down with Pamela one day, to discuss their relationship. Roberta feared that Pamela would begin a relationship with her birth mother before they had a chance to resolve their conflicts together. She was tired of wishing things could be different. There had to be something she could do.

Roberta's thoughts about her daughter were interrupted by the cab driver's horn. She grabbed her coat and carefully placed her right arm inside first. Roberta was very cautious about using her left arm, as that arm housed her fistula for dialysis. The fistula connected an artery to a vein in her left arm. It was this access that allowed the nurses to connect her to the machine which cleansed her blood of toxins. Most of the time, Roberta felt no pain on dialysis. She used a cream on her arm prior to the placement of the needles, and the dialysis nurses at Pioneer Valley were very skilled in inserting them. She was especially grateful for the care of her primary nurse, Joy, whose love for her work made everyone's day brighter. Although the needles didn't hurt, Roberta's pain was emotional. Her own mother's kidneys had failed due to polycystic kidney disease as well, but her mother was kept healthy on medication until her fiftieth birthday. Roberta had been diagnosed at thirty-nine. She felt cheated out of a decade of health. Roberta had fantasized throughout her life that her kidneys would function until she, too, turned fifty. No such luck, she mused. Roberta worried about her son being diagnosed as well. Thank goodness Pamela will not be plagued with this illness, Roberta sighed. The cab driver greeted her and she was driven to Ashland Street as his only passenger.

When Roberta arrived, she said hello to the receptionist, and sat in the waiting area. Her eyes averted the nutritionist, who often counseled Roberta about her large fluid gains and non-compliance with her renal diet and medications. I wasn't expecting to see her tonight, Roberta winced. Sheila was a tall, attractive woman about Roberta's age, with no weight problems at all. She was slender and well-dressed, and carried herself with poise and confidence. Sheila made attempts to communicate with Roberta, but each time, she failed to gain her trust. Sheila had approached the social worker, thinking that maybe she would be able to help.

When the nurses were ready for Roberta in the hemodialysis unit, the social worker was waiting to speak with her as well. Roberta attempted to avoid her stare. She had not spoken to the social worker about anything important since the onset of her treatment. Roberta even had trouble recalling her name. It was Laura, or Laurel, she thought.

"Hi, Roberta, how are you?"

"Just fine, thanks," Roberta announced in a perfunctory manner.

"You know you have Sheila worried," Laura remarked.

"I just can't stick to a diet. I've never been a disciplined person and it's just too restrictive."

"Do you notice any problems because of your fluid gains?"

"I'm always fatigued. And sometimes I have a hard time breathing."

"You'd feel better if you were more careful. Is there anything I can do to help?"

"I don't think so…"

Laura was attempting to assess whether or not Roberta experienced any secondary gains from her illness. Some patients with chronic illness chose to view themselves as sicker than others partly to be pampered at home or to establish in their own minds an identity as a disabled person. Others chose to deny their illness altogether, and were non-compliant because they convinced themselves they were well. End Stage Renal Disease produced complex emotional responses, and Laura always felt challenged by her job. It was a chronic illness with no cure which required life-sustaining treatment. Yet most patients did not look sick. Some maintained careers while on dialysis, and had full lives. Others practically gave up and deteriorated physically and emotionally. The factors which influenced people to enhance their ability to cope seemed to include having supportive families and strong faith. Laura knew little about Roberta's family, except for the superficial details.

"Is everything okay at home?" she asked.

Roberta decided to be honest. "Well, my daughter is thinking of going off to school in the fall," she started. "She does a lot for me at home and I'm a little worried. I'm trying to be happy for her, though. She's a smart kid and I think she'll do well."

Laura had met Pamela once, she recalled, when Roberta had started treatment. Laura was struck by her guarded, appeasing nature and her naivete. She guessed that Pamela was a slightly resentful caregiver.

"If we can help you stick to the diet, maybe you'd feel well enough to do more at home. Could there be some other reason you're having a hard time with the diet? Some people, women especially, tend to eat to avoid some difficult feelings."

"Well, I've certainly had my share of those. But I'm sure you don't want to hear about that."

"Actually, I do." Laura smiled. Maybe she could break through the barrier of Roberta's defensiveness.

"I'm frustrated a lot. I didn't think I'd be sick this early in my life. I don't think I want a transplant, but my mother keeps trying to convince me to be evaluated for the cadaver list. My husband is always working, and I never feel attractive anymore. And I'm constantly venting my anger at my daughter. It's like I can't help myself."

"What does she represent to you?"

Roberta's answer came quickly. "Health. She's slim and adorable. I decided to adopt her because I was afraid that my children would have polycystic kidney disease. But every time I look at her, I get angry about my own situation." Roberta sighed heavily as she thought about how her relationship had unfolded with her daughter. "Nelson made me the disciplinarian, because he was never home. When Pammy was small, I used to scream at her constantly. And even now, I criticize her. When I look at her, I see my own deficiencies. In September, she'll be leaving to start her own life, and I hardly know her. I'm afraid she'll search for her birth family and leave me behind. And why shouldn't she? I haven't been a very good mother to her. I haven't been fair to her."

"That's very sad, Roberta. Maybe you can tell her some of this before she leaves."

"I don't know..."

"Think about it. Maybe it would relieve some of your frustration if your relationship improves. You certainly seem to understand your behavior. You can decide to take more control in your life. You can choose to stop verbalizing your criticism in the same way as you choose to stop drinking too much fluid. What you're doing now isn't working, right? Maybe it's time for a change." Laura hoped Roberta would feel encouraged, not offended. "I bet if you stopped being so critical of yourself, you'd have an easier time with your daughter."

"I'll think about it," Roberta volunteered. And she did think about it. For the full four-hour treatment, Roberta remained wide-awake and planned her approach with Pamela. And she would try to stop the negative self-talk she had read about in self-help books. She would try to do as the books directed, and begin replacing negative messages with positive, nurturing messages. Roberta knew Laura was right. She was so critical of herself that it overflowed onto her daughter. It's not my fault that I'm sick, she professed. And I'm going to stop contributing to keeping myself sick. I'll start exercising again, a little bit at first. Maybe I'll join a gym. *It's not my fault that I'm sick*, Roberta affirmed again. *And it's certainly not Pamela's fault that she's healthy.*

Chapter 11

Pamela looked very pale when she stopped into Rachel's office.

"Are you all right?" Rachel asked. Pamela nodded. She sat on Rachel's couch, grabbed a pillow and clung to it with both arms, hugging it like a small doll against her heart.

"It's my birth mother, Ann Sullivan. She's dead."

"I'm so sorry, Pamela, what happened?"

"She was in a car accident. My father found her obituary in the paper. He called me at work because he thought the name sounded familiar, and he remembered that she lived in Connecticut. The obituary says that she is survived by her mother Leona Kenney, her husband Paul Sullivan, and her son, Paul Jr. I know this is a selfish reaction, but it hurt me that my name wasn't mentioned. I'm family, too. The funeral is tomorrow. I think I should go. Can I ask you something?"

"Of course."

"Are you adopted?"

"No, I'm not." Rachel thought of the many times after her mother's death that she had wished she were adopted. She wished for another father. He can't be my real father, someday I'll find my real father…"Why do you ask?"

"Well, you know a lot about it, and I thought…I think I'd like to meet some other people who are adopted. I don't know how to feel about this."

"There's no right way to feel, Pamela. Whatever you're feeling is okay."

"That's just it. I don't think I'm feeling anything. I know that an opportunity has ended for me, and I'll never get to know my birth mother. But I didn't know her. I just imagined her. I spoke to her once on the telephone. It's just so strange…I need to meet some other people who are dealing with this. Are there groups for people like me?"

"In fact, we're forming a group for adoptees that will meet here, every other Tuesday night."

"How do I join?"

"I'll speak with the facilitator. Her name is Judy. She's actually looking for some additional group members. With your permission, I'll give her your name and telephone numbers and she can let you know about the first scheduled meeting."

"Thanks, I would like that." Rachel was pleased that Pamela was reaching out in this way, instead of isolating herself again. "Do you think I'm crazy for going to the funeral?"

"No…"

"I just have a feeling about going. I want to make sure my brother is okay."

Pamela had asked Tracy to accompany her. Tracy had said she had no plans for the weekend. Pamela talked incessantly throughout the remainder of her session with Rachel. When her anxiety level was high, Pamela became very loquacious. Because of her confusion about her birth mother's death, Pamela neglected to tell Rachel about her acceptance to Antioch.

In the morning, Pamela donned a simple black velour dress and drove to Tracy's house. Tracy called to her from upstairs when Pamela arrived. She had gotten off to a slow start this morning and was not yet ready to leave. Pamela climbed the staircase to the second floor of Tracy's house. The stairway wall was covered with family photographs. Pamela found herself staring at one in particular. It was a photograph of Tracy as a young girl, blowing out the candles atop a large birthday cake. The cake was covered in white icing, with pink and green flowers encircling the candles. Tracy's mother stood behind her, with her hands lovingly placed on her daughter's shoulders. Tracy's grandmother was kneeling at her granddaughter's side. Three generations of women celebrating another birthday together. Three generations of women with similar smiles and faces filled with anticipation. Pamela continued to stare at the photograph. She thought of herself, Ann Sullivan, and Leona Kenney. For the first time since she received the news about Ann Kenney Sullivan, her eyes filled with tears.

Pamela had never been to a cemetery before. The grounds were immaculate. They decided to wait in the car, and Pamela followed a small procession of people walking slowly toward the burial plot of her mother. She spotted her brother, Paul, and was shocked to find him walking with crutches, with a cast on his left leg. He wore a neck brace as well. *He was in the car with her*, Pamela thought. She could not bring herself to talk to him. She didn't belong here. No one knew who she was. Pamela began to have second thoughts about her choice to attend the funeral. She felt dizzy suddenly, and leaned against a large oak tree to regain her balance. Pamela chose not to walk any closer. She could hear the eulogy for Ann Kenney Sullivan, who was described as a devoted wife and mother, gone too soon. Paul Sullivan, Jr. seemed to be absorbed in his own thoughts. He looked handsome in his attire, even with his head stiff from the neck brace. Pamela stood facing him, in the distance, wondering how he was coping with this sudden tragedy. Had he been conscious when his mother died? Did he say goodbye? Pamela wanted to comfort him. She stood paralyzed, leaning against the tree for support. After the coffin was placed in the ground, the crowd began to disperse slowly. It was then that Pamela noticed her brother staring at her. He looked as if he had seen a ghost. Paul Sullivan, Jr. slowly hobbled over to where Pamela stood. He seemed transfixed by her face.

"Who are you?" he questioned.

"My name is Pamela Windsor."

"Paul Sullivan. I'm sorry…I'm staring. You look just like my mother. Did you know her?"

"Just briefly. I'm sorry for your loss."

"Thanks. How did you know my Mom?"

Pamela thought about lying. Maybe lying in certain circumstances was the best option. Ann Sullivan had not wanted her son to know about the adoption. Pamela had attended the funeral to be certain that her brother was okay. She had accomplished her goal. His life should be her primary concern. He had just lost his mother.

"I'm a coworker of hers."

"My Mom didn't work."

"I'm sorry, I don't think your Mom would want me to be here."

"Who are you?"

"I'm your half-sister. I was adopted as an infant."

"I thought so! My grandmother told me I had a sister. She just told me about you last year. My grandmother asked me not to talk to my Mom, but I bugged her all the time anyway about being an only child, hoping she would tell me. She never did. How did you find us?"

Pamela was speechless for a few moments. *He knows about me!* "Through the adoption agency. I spoke with your mother for the first time a few weeks ago."

"*Our* mother," Paul corrected her. "Grandma Lee says they named you Joelle. I thought that was a pretty name. But I guess they changed it when you were adopted. I had no idea how to find you. Do you live around here?"

"West Springfield." *Joelle. It was a pretty name.*

"Do you want to meet Grandma Lee? She's pretty upset about Mom."

"No, I don't think I should, not today."

"Will you call me? I have to go back to the house."

" I have your number." Pamela reached into her handbag for a pen and paper, and wrote down her telephone numbers for Paul Sullivan.

'Thanks for coming today, Pamela. I'll call you!"

Paul touched Pamela's shoulder while balancing on his crutches. She responded self-consciously by kissing his cheek, and blushed. Pamela turned to leave, looking back to observe her family. Once she entered Tracy's Toyota, she did not stop talking until they were back in West Springfield. Pamela was most incredulous about the fact that her brother knew who she was, and that he *wanted* to know her. It seemed as if her grandmother might want to know her as well. Pamela was thrilled!

Her mother was sitting in the kitchen when Pamela entered the house. "Pammy, your father told me about Ann Sullivan. Are you okay?"

"I'm fine, thanks. I just met my half-brother, and I think I might be able to meet my maternal grandmother."

"Do you have a minute to sit down?"

Pamela sat with her mother at the kitchen table. Her mother was finishing a healthy lunch. Mrs. Windsor told Pamela that she had been doing a lot of thinking about their relationship. She wanted things to be better between them. She knew she had been critical of Pamela in the past, and she apologized. She was trying to change. Mrs. Windsor told Pamela that she was sorry about her birth mother, and that she wanted to be a better mother to her.

"I've started shopping and vacuuming again, Pammy, I don't want you to have to do that anymore. I'm feeling better since I'm following my diet, and watching my fluid intake. I have more energy, and I've met some really nice people in my support group."

"Can you stop calling me Pammy?"

"You're a grown woman, headed for college, I can certainly start calling you Pamela."

Hallelujah! Pamela thought. She heard me. "Thanks!" Pamela rose and climbed the stairs to her bedroom. Judy from Access Health Center had called. Pamela returned the call and was given the information about the adoptees group. She planned to attend the first meeting on Tuesday.

On Sunday morning, Pamela remembered an incident that had receded to the back of her conscious mind for years. Pamela's mother had gotten angry with her, and was pulling her hair. They stood at the top of the stairway, Pamela struggling to release herself from her mother's grip. She remembered being slapped across the face, and losing her balance. She fell down a flight of stairs, bruising her elbows and knees badly. A bump formed on the back of her head. Her mother put some ice in a washcloth and applied it to each bruised area, apologizing profusely for hitting her. Years later, Brian had slapped her face as well. But there was more to that story, that only Pamela's mother knew. During that argument in the car, after slapping her, Brian kept driving. He was driving up the hill to his house, reached over to Pamela's door, pushed it open, and pushed her out onto the street. The bruises on her elbows and knees reappeared. She was fortunate, because neither incident produced any broken bones. She assumed there were no fractures, either. Neither her mother nor Brian thought about medical attention for her. Both of them had been violent. And both of them had affected her opinion of herself, and of how she deserved to be treated.

When Pamela arrived home, limping, from the incident with Brian, her mother stood at the front door. "What the hell happened to you? Did you let that boyfriend of yours do this to you? What the hell is wrong with you?"

It was the only time in Pamela's life that she confronted her mother about the years of abuse. "That boyfriend of mine must have taken lessons from you!" The memory still stung. It still caused Pamela to feel the deep betrayal she had grown accustomed to associating with her mother. Pamela was extremely doubtful about trusting her mother's change of heart. The apology was nice, but she had heard those words before. If Pamela ever had children, she promised herself that she would never lift a hand to hurt them. And as for Brian, she hoped never to see him again. Some things were just unforgivable.

Chapter 12

Rachel had very little time to think about the effect of Pamela's birth mother's death. She was shaken by their session, and knew that Pamela would soon be experiencing every emotion imaginable. It seemed to take a while before Pamela integrated events on an emotional level. She was able to deal with each crisis, albeit anxiously, before her emotions crept onto the scene to create their chaos. Rachel was sure that this modus operandi had served Pamela well throughout her life. Rachel was even slightly envious of the way in which Pamela's defenses worked. Rachel's feelings rose to the surface immediately in the midst of the most intense crisis. She could not control them.

There was a message in Rachel's mailbox from Glen. He had called her at work and requested that she contact him as soon as possible. Rachel called home. Glen answered the phone on the first ring.

"Rachel, honey, you got a message on the answering machine from a law clerk at the Office of the Public Administrator in Nassau County. I hope you don't mind, but I thought it was important and I called Long Island myself.

"What is it?" Rachel grew anxious. There was only one relative left in Nassau County.

"It's your father. The police found him dead, and the law clerk said he died intestate. That means without a will. The Public Administrator's office is searching for relatives to identify him and to claim his property.

They need you to go to New York with your birth certificate. Honey? Are you okay?"

Rachel was feeling surprisingly clear-headed. A little like Pamela, she thought. She was certain her clarity had to do with her history with her father. The lack of love. The neglect and abuse. It was finally over. The only place her father would exist now was in her mind, and Rachel was improving her ability to control those intrusions. "I'm okay, Glen. Thank you for calling New York for me. I'll drive down tomorrow to take care of things."

"I was nervous about calling you, Rachel. You probably knew it was something urgent from the message, because I never call you at work." Rachel heard the relief in his voice. "Do you want me to come to New York with you?"

"I think I should ask Aunt Lynn to accompany me, love. My mother's things are still in that house, and I think she'd want to be there."

Rachel ended the call and saw one additional client. She remained remarkably calm throughout the session. She asked Hilary to cancel her other appointments for the evening and the next few days. Rachel remembered that Pamela would most likely be attending the adoption group meeting this week, and was glad that she would have support in case the New York trip took longer than expected.

Rachel discovered that her father had died of liver disease. He had sought no medical attention. He died alone in his living room. Empty liquor bottles stood to attest to his condition. In the end, they were his only friends, the only witnesses to his demise. Rachel felt a pang of pity for the man she hardly knew, her father, whose disease had warped his reasoning and contributed to his violence for so many years. In that moment, her father became merely a sick man to Rachel, and the monster image of her childhood vanished. She would no longer be his victim. He was a broken man who had been a victim himself. He had no more power over her. Rachel and Aunt Lynn identified his body at the morgue. They arranged to have it cremated, as neither of them could stomach the idea of burying him next to Janine Andrews Abbott for eternity. They collected the belongings worth saving from the home in Wantagh. They filled the trunk of the car with boxes to take with them to Massachusetts. They spoke with a lawyer. Bank accounts were closed. They worked hard for several days, packing bags of household items and clothing to bring to charities. Rachel and Aunt Lynn both reopened the wound of Janine's death, as their chores were constant reminders of the life she lived. The house had to be cleaned as well, and the two women scrubbed areas that had not seen a sponge for years. The furniture was fittingly donated to a nearby battered women's shelter. When the house was empty, Aunt Lynn called a realtor. She arranged to pay a monthly fee so that the house could be maintained until it was sold. The realtor arrived with her FOR SALE sign, planting the post in the ground in the front yard. Rachel signed a contract. At thirty-two years old, she was now an orphan.

On the way home to Massachusetts, the news on the radio was grim. NATO forces had been bombing Kosovo, and many refugees were facing horrific conditions at the area's borders. Some children had been separated from their parents. Some were old and very sick. Food, sanitation and shelter were scarce. Reporters interpreted stories about destruction and murder. Rachel felt very grateful for her life in the United States. She glanced over at her wonderful Aunt Lynn, and reached for her hand.

"I love you, Aunt Lynn. Thank you for coming to Long Island with me. All of my decisions were easier with you there to help."

Aunt Lynn smiled, squeezed Rachel's hand, and closed her eyes to sleep. The trip had exhausted her, and Rachel knew her way home.

* * * * * * * * * * * * * * * * *

Rachel arrived home in a very amorous mood. She had missed Glen, as they were seldom apart. She was accustomed to his arms encircling her small frame during the night, the sound of his breathing, the pulse of his heartbeat against her back. It had been difficult to sleep in her old bedroom on Long Island without him. Rachel had called him several times and rushed through their telephone conversations, as there had been so much to accomplish in a short time. Now that her father was gone, she felt more determined than ever not to let her memory interfere with her sexuality. Tonight, she would push herself to her limits with her husband.

Glen looked thrilled to see her, and she fell into his open arms. He had set the table in the dining room and had lit two candles. Rachel was not yet hungry for dinner, and Glen recognized her need immediately. He began to kiss her neck softly as they embraced. She pulled his face toward hers and kissed him passionately, teasing his lips with her tongue. She unbuttoned his shirt and reached beneath it to caress his muscular chest. She whispered her love for him. For a moment, Rachel pulled away and reached over to the stereo. Instrumental music filled the room. Then she surprised herself. Rachel dimmed the lights. She was determined not to fear the dark any longer. After her eyes adjusted themselves, Rachel was pleased to learn that she could still see Glen clearly. There would be no mistaking him for her father, ever again. Rachel welcomed the sensual darkness, moving closer to Glen, melding her pelvis with his in a slow, purposeful dance. She reached for Glen's arms, and pulled his hands toward her breasts, her desire for him mounting. As he massaged her breasts, teasing each nipple to rise, she whispered to her husband.

"I want you to undress me."

Glen had never heard this request from his wife before. She found his questioning look endearing. She moved his fingers to the top of her blouse to wordlessly confirm her request. Glen realized then that his wife was ready to give herself to him, and this knowledge excited him immensely. Somehow tonight would be different. Glen met his wife's passion with his own, kissing her with force and desire. His breath grew heavier. Rachel allowed a soft moan to escape her throat. She was present. She was experiencing this sweet moment with her dear husband with no distraction.

"I want you." she whispered.

Glen continued undressing her until she stood naked before him. She felt herself becoming moist with anticipation. Rachel took Glen's hand and walked him to the couch, removing the remainder of his clothing before he sat down. She knelt in front of him, and with her tongue, she brought her husband to the peak of ecstasy. She rose to join him on the couch, straddling him carefully. She gave her breasts to his mouth, and closed her eyes to enjoy the intensity of her nipples hardening in response to his insistent lips and tongue. Glen put his hands on her waist, slowly lowering her torso so that he could enter her. He could feel her readiness for him. Rachel's body stiffened. Glen thought he had been too aggressive. But this night *was* different. Rachel allowed only the tip of his penis to enter her, teasing him mercilessly with her movements until he thought he could bear it no longer. He whispered her name. Rachel obliged by relaxing her legs in a final effort to please her husband, rising and falling with his rhythm until he climaxed inside of her.

Afterwards, Rachel turned in his lap and felt his warm fingers begin to caress her moist center. He moved them in a circular motion, exploring her expertly until he found the core of her excitement. Rachel's pelvis seemed to move involuntarily to the rhythm of his touch, and she could feel the sensual heat rising inside of her. The new sensations she felt were pleasant, but gradually, her body betrayed her once again. Her excitement abated and finally, the sensations evaporated. She reached for Glen's hand in an effort to stop its movement. The once-pleasurable feelings had become painful. *How ironic*, she thought.

Prior to her father's abuse, Rachel had provided pleasure to herself on many pubescent nights. After the incest started, it was as if her father had stolen the warm feelings from the core of her being. She despised the term frigid, but knew many colleagues who might apply it to her condition. She was not frigid. She was stuck in the mire of her father's crimes against her. She prayed for emotional and physical release, if only to stop her husband from feeling that he was inadequate as a lover. He never spoke about it, but Rachel was certain that his self-esteem had been eroded by his perceived lack of ability to please her. And he was such a wonderful partner! Carrying the baggage of her history was unfair to him as well.

"You're a wonderful lover," she told Glen. "It's me. You took me further than I've ever climbed tonight, honey."

"You made some changes. It almost seems as though your father's death made you feel free."

"You noticed?"

"The lights, undressing you, of course I noticed! You were more open to me."

"I felt that way. You always impress me with how perceptive you are."

Glen changed the subject. Rachel was grateful. He continued to embrace her, and talked about wanting to take a trip, a vacation with her. He had loved the visits he had made to the west, especially to the national parks, and had been wanting to plan a vacation to Arizona or Utah. He loved to photograph the amazing red rocks in the glory of a sunrise or sunset, and he wanted to share the experience of places like Bryce Canyon with his wife. It had been so long since they had been away together, and he thought it would be a nice change for Rachel, especially after dealing with her father's death.

Rachel found herself agreeing. The usual thoughts that entered her mind about work and commitment to her patients in crisis paled next to her new resolve. She had seen the photographs her husband had collected from past trips. Waterfalls in Yosemite, red rocks in Zion National Park, the Grand Canyon. Glen seemed to express his spirituality through his photographs. They often reminded Rachel of images of heaven. The photographs seemed unreal to her, breathtaking and awesome. She wanted to travel with Glen to places she had never been.

Their intimacy and tenderness after lovemaking always touched a place in Rachel's soul. Maybe she could connect more deeply to her spirituality as Glen took his photographs. She would help him to plan the trip. Perhaps she could take several weeks off in July.

"Let's do it!" She told her husband. And in that moment, loving Glen meant more to Rachel than work had ever meant in the past.

Chapter 13

When Pamela saw Rachel again, she was determined not to ask any personal questions of her therapist. She was curious about Rachel, and wanted to ask how she was feeling, but knew this was not supposed to be a relationship which included reciprocity. Rachel looked well. The receptionist had explained to Pamela when she called to cancel her counseling appointment that there had been a death in Rachel's family. Pamela began the session with Rachel by talking about the adoption group. It had gone wonderfully, and Pamela had been thrilled to meet other adoptees who were coping with the same issues about identity as she was. Some had conducted successful searches, some had not been interested in finding their birth families at all. She had been astounded to meet young men who were emotionally vulnerable in the group. One in particular had been having a great deal of trouble in relationships with women. He found it difficult to be intimate with women, and even spoke of sexual intimacy. His biggest fear was that he could be sleeping with a relative, and not even know it! In his mind, he knew the chances of having sex with a sister or cousin would be incredibly unlikely, but he obsessed about it nonetheless. The only information he had been given about his adoption was that his birth parents had had too many children to be able to take care of him as well. He was plagued by this notion of a large family, and Judy had helped him to connect this information from his family with his problems in relationships. This particular young man had recently chosen to lead a life of celibacy until he completed his adoption search. It was the only way he could rid himself of his 'adoption anxiety', as he referred to it.

The group members had confronted Pamela about her lack of feeling about her birth mother's recent death. Pamela had tried to explain that meeting her brother and knowing about her grandmother had overshadowed the death of her birth mother. The group had not been convinced. With prompting, Pamela was later able to acknowledge some anger at her birth mother, for rejecting contact with her and for hurting her brother. Pamela had assumed that the accident was a result of the reckless driving she had witnessed in Connecticut. In actuality, though, she had no information about the accident, and was not sure that she wanted to know anything. Pamela's brother had called her, and they had planned to meet in Springfield for dinner. Finally, Pamela could bear it no longer.

"They told me you had a death in your family," she announced to Rachel. "Are you okay?"

"I'm fine." Rachel answered.

"I know I shouldn't be asking, but were you close to the person who died?"

"It was my father who died, and I hadn't seen him in many years."

"Is your mother okay?"

"My mother died when I was a little girl."

"I'm so sorry! I shouldn't have opened my big mouth! I didn't mean to be nosey!"

"It's okay, Pamela. I'm doing fine. And I don't think you're being nosey. I think you merely need to reassure yourself that I'm okay, and that I can continue to listen well to your concerns. It was the first time that I canceled a session with you. It's rare that I cancel with such short notice, and it makes sense that you're curious about it. And there's something else, Pamela. You're used to being the emotional caretaker in your family. Your father expects that you'll take care of him emotionally when you're not getting along with your mother. And your mother expects the same from you when she's feeling sad or angry. It must be very hard for you to focus on yourself and your concerns when your inclination is to take care of me, too."

"Well, that all makes perfect sense. But I am sorry about your losses. I do care about how you are. The relationship is so one-sided. It's very contrived, in a way. It's hard sometimes to talk to you about such personal things and not know anything at all about you. I wish I could reciprocate in some way for all you've done for me."

Pamela listened as Rachel explained a bit about the theory behind the 'blank slate' of the therapist's persona. She appreciated the fact that Rachel never acted condescending with her, and that her explanations always helped alleviate Pamela's concerns. Rachel often tried to clarify the purpose and benefits of counseling. Pamela was certain she was changing. She was getting to know herself, and starting to like who she was.

Pamela was so positively affected by her individual and group counseling experiences that she had started formulating a new goal. She would find a way to help other adoptees like herself. Pamela would continue to get to know her own birth family. She was hopeful about feeling satisfied with the outcome of her search. Once she reached that point, she would find a way to communicate with others about the psychology of adoption in the way that Rachel had so effectively communicated with her.

* * * * * * * * * * * * * * * * * *

The dinner with Paul went well. Pamela was talkative and friendly, and her brother seemed to be interested in every word she said. His face lit up when she mentioned Keene, New Hampshire, because he had a good friend in high school who recently moved there. Paul Sullivan was driven to the restaurant by a young woman who Pamela had noticed at the funeral, his girlfriend Denise. He still wore the cast on his leg, and seemed to get around on his crutches with ease now. Her brother was well-built, with dark hair and blue eyes much like her own. She was embarrassed to acknowledge to herself that she found him attractive. Pamela thought of the young man from the adoptee's group. What if she *had* met her brother in another context, and the chemistry between them was like it was now? Paul introduced Pamela to his girlfriend Denise, and she was charming. Paul seemed mature for his age. He spoke about their mother, and answered Pamela's questions without hesitation. He had brought some family photographs with him, and gave Pamela a photograph of himself and Denise on the night of their Junior Prom. He was startlingly handsome in his dark brown tuxedo, and Pamela knew she would treasure the photo.

The waitress had visited their table several times before they were ready to order, and they finally decided on the same entrée together. Every aspect of their lives was dissected for similarities. They seemed to have similar tastes in food, and took the opportunity to discuss the menu items in detail in order to determine this truth. They laughed in all the same places. Paul spoke of wanting to go to college to become a veterinarian, and was not surprised that Pamela shared his love for animals. They even had similar mannerisms when they spoke, using their hands and arms freely to communicate. Paul cocked his head to one side when he listened intently. Pamela had never even realized she did that also, until she saw herself in him. *So this is what family feels like*, she thought. How wonderful to grow up with the privilege of being similar to the people around you! At one point, Pamela began to get tearful. Paul acknowledged the change in her mood right away. He asked about her life, her adoptive family, how the adoption had affected her. He was so comforting to her. The tears that she shed in saying goodbye to him that evening were tears of joy, for having found him, as well as tears of sorrow, for having been without him for so long. She knew they had cemented their relationship this evening. He was a part of her life now. Her birth mother's death had made that possible. Rachel had said that in every crisis lies an opportunity. Pamela was beginning to understand the irony of life.

* * * * * * * * * * * * * * * * * *

Paul called Pamela at work the following week. Not only to tell her that he enjoyed their dinner together, but he had an idea. He had spoken with his friend Kyle in New Hampshire. Kyle's parents ran a summer camp for children, and they were looking for counselors. Kyle had offered interviews to both Denise and Paul, and Paul had told him about Pamela. Paul thought she could work as a counselor in New Hampshire prior to starting school. She could get to know the area and meet new people. It would be easier for her to find an apartment if she lived in the camp's facilities for the summer. He told her the salary range for the counselor position, and Pamela calculated quickly. Financially, she could afford it, especially because the counselors' salaries included room and board. The idea of spending the summer with her brother was very appealing.

"I have to think about it, Paul. Work out the details. But it sounds like a great plan."

Paul sounded pleased with her response and offered her the telephone number to contact Kyle's parents directly. His interview was scheduled for Saturday, May 8th, and he thought she had time to arrange hers on the same day. They could travel together. The children did not arrive at camp until July, but there was an Orientation Program that started in June for all counselors. Since they offered a thorough training program, they did not require prior camp counseling experience. Pamela jotted down the telephone number. She could always call to schedule the interview, and cancel it if she changed her mind.

Some things seemed to fall into place very naturally. She would miss Tracy, and of course, her father. She would miss seeing Rachel every week, but she could write to her and schedule sessions whenever she visited Massachusetts. Pamela loved children, and thought it would be a great opportunity to work at a camp. She telephoned the number on her desk, and identified herself as Paul's sister. She was greeted warmly by Kyle's mother and given more detailed information about the positions available. There were specialty counselors needed. Did she have any special interests or skills? Could she teach Arts and Crafts, or Swimming? Pamela mentioned her interest in the environment and her plans to attend Antioch in the fall. Maybe she could coordinate some nature walks, or hikes with the children. Kyle's mother liked the idea. Pamela scheduled an interview for May 8th as well, and grew more excited as she realized the plan might actually be a plausible one.

Her parents were surprised about the suddenness of her decision. They questioned her desire to move so abruptly, and reminded Pamela that June was only weeks away. Was she sure it was best to leave her job? Pamela explained that she hadn't made any decisions yet, but wanted to follow through with the interview. That logic sounded reasonable to her parents. Pamela kept her other thoughts to herself. She knew her parents wouldn't understand. *I feel like I've known my brother for a long time, yet we just met. I trust him. Something about him assures me that his intentions are good. He seems so genuine. He's got the same idealism and enthusiasm that I hear in my own heart. My connection with him feels solid and mystical at the same time. Old and new. I hope I get this job. I want to spend the summer in New Hampshire with my brother, Paul Sullivan, Jr.*

* * * * * * * * * * * * * * * * * *

The eighth day of May was filled with the sounds and colors of spring in New England. The drive to New Hampshire was beautiful, and Pamela found that she was able to appreciate the scenery anew. The drive to Antioch with her father had been tense because of her mood after the initial contact with her birth mother. This trip was different. Pamela enjoyed Paul and Denise's company immensely. She felt right at home.

Once they reached the site of the camp, they found that only one cabin had been opened for the season. They stepped inside, and Pamela found the western décor cozy. Large rugs hung from the walls, and they took seats on a Mission-style couch surrounded by pillows depicting buffalo and bison. A desk in the office area housed a computer which had Internet access. An advertisement on the monitor awaited a response from the computer's owner. Kyle's mother, Mrs. Emily Tobin, introduced herself to the triad on her couch. She met with them each one by one, and each returned to the couch impressed with her presentation about the camp. Denise was a member of her high school's varsity swim team, and chose to apply for the specialty position. She was also a trained lifeguard, and could teach lifesaving skills. Paul was sports-minded and was thrilled to discover all of the sports equipment the camp had purchased. He had even noticed a kayak he hoped he could try out in a nearby lake, after his cast was removed. Pamela was impressed with Mrs. Tobin's down-to-earth nature, her friendliness and openness about the hiring process. This was the first interview Pamela had completed without one ounce of anxiety. Mrs. Tobin announced that they would each be hearing from her within the week, and thanked them for coming.

* * * * * * * * * * * * * * * * * *

Pamela came striding into Rachel's office. She carried a letter which she read aloud to Rachel, announcing her job offer at Camp Winnepeg. She would need to relocate by June 26th, and begin their orientation and training program before the children arrived. Rachel heard the enthusiasm in Pamela's voice, and they discussed her joy about finding her brother. They talked about Pamela preparing to meet Paul's grandmother – her grandmother – and all of the feelings that accompanied so much newness and change. Pamela was in very good spirits, and seemed to Rachel to be more confident than ever. She was utilizing the positive input she received from her relationship with her brother to enhance her self-esteem. She was incorporating her new perception of family into a new view of herself. Pamela had stopped making self-deprecating comments. She had alleviated a great deal of her anxiety. She seldom became apologetic about her words or actions anymore. As Rachel listened, she realized that Pamela was ready to spread her wings in New Hampshire. The once-fragile bird had become a soaring eagle, ready to handle the new challenges of young adult life. No longer isolated or afraid, Pamela would leave counseling in a few weeks to *become* a counselor. How fitting, Rachel mused.

Rachel broached the subject of termination of treatment with caution. Rachel knew it would be difficult to lose Pamela as a client. She enjoyed being able to witness her process of self-actualization, and would miss their contact. Rachel hoped Pamela would continue to keep in touch. Pamela respectfully spoke about the meaning that counseling held for her, and reiterated her desire to continue to schedule occasional appointments. She promised to write. Although there would be several sessions prior to their last, this meeting was the most vulnerable for Pamela. She expressed to Rachel that she was like the mother Pamela always wanted. She would never forget Rachel, nor her unconditional support and guidance during a very difficult time in her life. She had a 'Rachel voice' in her head now, and it helped her to nurture herself and smooth over her anxiety and sadness. And Pamela told Rachel about her wish to help other adoptees. She would find a way to share her experiences in order to aid others.

Rachel shared as much as she could appropriately risk regarding her feelings about ending. Rachel said that she had learned a lot from Pamela, and that she enjoyed working with her. She did not have the clarity of mind that accompanied most of her terminations with clients, however. This time was more difficult. When Pamela left the room,

Rachel allowed herself her sadness. *You've been a bit like a daughter to me, too, Pamela. I'll miss you, little bird.*

Chapter 14

The first letter from Pamela arrived in Rachel's mailbox in July. Rachel had been wondering about Pamela, and was hopeful that her summer was going well. Although Rachel missed working with her, she trusted that Pamela wanted their contact to continue. The letter she was holding was proof of that.

Dear Rachel,

I'm really glad I decided to take this job for the summer. Everyone here is really friendly and nice, and the kids are great! I know I'm biased, but my brother is a great guy with a lot of charisma. He makes friends easily and can joke around, but he has a very genuine and serious side, too. His grandmother is coming to the camp to visit in a few weeks. I'm finally going to meet her. I'm a little nervous about that but Paul keeps reassuring me that it'll be fine. I think I'm finally settling into the knowledge that I have two families. That's not so bad…

And…I met someone! His name is Dylan and he's one of the Assistant Directors here. He's into computers and I've been learning about the Internet with his help. I told him about being adopted. I've been able to tell him a lot about myself, even about my counseling and my abortion. He's easygoing and treats me really well. Actually, that seems to be a problem. I guess I got used to the way Brian treated me, and it's hard to believe that I deserve anything more. I'm working on it though! I keep hearing things you've said to me and I know in my head that I deserve all that I'm willing to give. I just have to get my heart to follow along.

Dylan says that he could help me develop a way to communicate with other adoptees via computer. I could have my own web site. Dylan studied computers at college and he's starting a job in the fall here in New Hampshire.

I don't ever remember feeling so good about my life. I feel like I'm finally in charge, and making some good decisions. I know my time in counseling was short, and there's a lot more to think about, but I really feel like you helped me tremendously. Thank you again.

That's all the news from here, I guess. I hope you miss seeing me every week! I miss the group members, too. I'm still in touch with some of them. I hope to visit after camp is over and before school starts. I'll keep in touch.

Sincerely,

Pamela Windsor

Rachel folded the letter neatly into its envelope. As her day progressed, she thought of Pamela. How different she sounded than when she first began counseling. Just six months had passed, but a great deal had changed in her life. And in Rachel's life as well. Tomorrow, Rachel and Glen would be boarding a plane to Salt Lake City together. And instead of feeling tense and anxious about leaving work, Rachel felt joyous about the idea of a vacation shared with her husband. A new concept, but one that was starting to sit well with her. She planned to leave work earlier than usual in order to finish packing. Glen wanted to take her out to dinner. He had recently been promoted at work and wanted to celebrate. The day passed slowly. Rachel tried to focus on the issues her clients were presenting, but grew distracted in her thoughts about Pamela, and about Utah. During her three o'clock break, Rachel discovered two messages in her mailbox from the receptionist. Her last two clients had canceled their sessions! Rachel took time to write her progress notes, and smiling from ear to ear, practically jogged out of the office to her car.

"See you in a few weeks!" she told Hilary.

* * * * * * * * * * * * * * * * *

Glen had booked a direct flight from Boston to Salt Lake City. With their backpacks in the trunk of his car, Glen drove to Boston via the Mass Pike. He had made dinner reservations at Legal Seafood, one of his wife's favorite restaurants. The drive to Boston included talk of their itinerary, and Rachel still could not erase the smile from her lips.

Her lobster dinner was delicious, and the restaurant's ambiance was very romantic. Her husband removed a small velvet jewelry box from his jacket pocket. Rachel looked quizzically at him.

"What's this?"

"Part of the celebration. Open it."

Rachel loved antique jewelry. Inside, Glen had placed a magnificent estate piece, a ring that appeared to be of exceptional quality. It was a small diamond in a filigree setting of white gold, surrounded by two sapphires. He could tell by her expression that he had made the right choice.

"Glen, this is the most beautiful ring I've ever seen!"

"Try it on."

Rachel placed the ring on her right index finger, and it fit perfectly. She loved the look of it. "It's perfect!"

"You're always surprising me with gifts, sweetheart. I wanted to find something that expressed how special you are to me. You're my dearest friend, and I love being married to you."

Rachel continued to smile as her eyes grew moist. "I love you, Glen." The couple held hands and could easily have been mistaken for newlyweds all evening.

* * * * * * * * * * * * * * * * * *

Rachel had had few opportunities to travel in her life. She had lived in New York and Massachusetts, and had no criteria for judging the vastness and beauty of the western United States. Glen rented a car at the airport. They were exhausted from the long flight, and hardly noticed anything about the hotel room he had reserved for them. They quickly undressed and slipped beneath the cool sheets of the king-sized bed. They held each other close. Rachel fell into a sound, tranquil sleep.

The drive to Bryce Canyon was filled with sights Rachel had never seen. Everything looked different to her. The architecture, the sky, the mountains, the desert. Even the colors seemed brighter. She wondered if she simply felt more relaxed on vacation, and was therefore more able than usual to admire the beauty of nature. No, she decided, there was more to appreciate. Life felt sacred here. Glen did all the driving. He was very much at peace in their rented convertible, top down, wind in his hair, radio blaring, traveling south with his wife by his side.

Bryce Canyon was even more scenic than Glen's photographs portrayed. Rachel began to feel the kind of spiritual peace that Glen had always described to her about the area. Her problems seemed so little here; her past like a fleeting second in time. She was basking in the glory of the place, when Glen whispered to her.

"There's a hiking trail up there. Feel like hiking?"

They emerged from the car in awe. Glen had found a trail he was familiar with, and took Rachel's hand. They climbed and walked and wandered, noticing chipmunks, tiny lizards and desert flowers along the way. People were friendly, and they conversed with travelers from different parts of the country. Others spoke languages that sounded unfamiliar to them, and Rachel realized that people traveled to this spot from all over the world. Carrying cameras and broad smiles, they seemed as awestruck by the canyon as Rachel was. As the trail widened, Rachel put her arm around her husband's waist. He held her close in response, and they continued their journey. The sun and clouds created beautiful designs of light and dark on the red rocks. The trail ended in a place where they could view a great portion of the canyon at once. Rachel and Glen sat in silence as the sun began to set. Rachel rested her head on Glen's shoulder, feeling a tranquility that she had never known.

That night, they stayed near Bryce Canyon and prepared for traveling to Arizona the following day. Glen had wanted his wife to see Sedona, as well as the Grand Canyon and the Painted Desert. He did an enormous amount of driving, but appeared not to be exhausted by it. There were so few cars on the road in comparison to the east. He said that driving was actually a pleasurable experience here.

Although Rachel loved Arizona, it was later in the week, having traveled north to Colorado, that she fell in love with Boulder. Pearl Street reminded her of Main Street in Northampton, except that the Rocky Mountains were spectacular. She understood the word 'breathtaking' differently now. She had seen magical scenery in Colorado that actually took her breath away. They had rented bicycles, basked in the sun, ate wonderful, healthy dinners. It was the best vacation Rachel had ever had.

Glen had saved Yellowstone National Park for last. The following week, the drive into Wyoming seemed to take forever. Passing through old western towns, Rachel felt that time had stood still. Glen drove through Grand Teton National Park, and upon arriving in Yellowstone, Rachel was awestruck again. The car had nearly come to a halt, as a small herd of bison slowly strolled across the path of the traveling tourists. Rachel had been to the Bronx Zoo, but had never seen animals in their natural habitat. Glen pointed out a bear which was hardly visible in the hills ahead. They stopped the car to witness Old Faithful, and sat on the benches provided to await the geiser's activity. The geiser was an amazing sight to behold. Afterwards, Rachel and Glen walked arm and arm, joined for a few minutes by a group of elk strolling alongside them.

"I'll never forget this trip, Glen. Thank you so much for planning it for us."

"I'm glad you feel that way, Rachel. Maybe you'll come back here with me, now that you've seen what it's like."

"Of course I will!"

Glen took a series of photographs for the remainder of the day. They wandered through the mammoth hot springs, and later, saw a beautiful waterfall. The landscape continued to astound Rachel. They had a last dinner together in Wyoming, and Glen drove to Billings, Montana that evening. They would leave from the airport in the morning.

Rachel discovered with the sunrise why Montana is called the Big Sky state. They drove to the airport, and returned their rental car. Although it cost a fortune to rent a car in one state and return it in another, Glen had known it was the best way to introduce Rachel to the west. She had to agree with him. She had enjoyed the trip so immensely that she fought tears when she boarded the plane home. Glen noticed her mood change, as usual.

"We'll come back, love," he said, "I promise."

* * * * * * * * * * * * * * * * *

A second letter from Pamela awaited Rachel. This envelope was thicker. Rachel placed it inside her briefcase. She wanted to be able to read it in its entirety during her break, instead of rushing through it between sessions. She invited her client into her office, and began her first day back at Access Health Center.

Her break came at noon. Rachel sat in the employee lounge, alone, and read.

Dear Rachel,

I guess things were going too well. I missed my period. I took a birth control test yesterday and sure enough, I'm pregnant (again). I told Dylan and he's reeling from the news. We were careful...most of the time.

Rachel, I don't think I can have another abortion. I know the timing is awful, but I would really like to have this baby. I could still start school in September, at least for the first semester. Dylan managed to say that he really wants to be a Dad, but we hardly know each other. He's twenty-three, just starting a new career. He's worried about money, but he's willing to think about living together after camp is over. We'd see how it worked out. If we don't make it, I could always go back home and deal with the fallout from my parents' reactions. Somehow, this life inside me feels paramount.

I know I worked hard to figure out what I wanted to do with college and stuff, but I might be just as happy if I could make things work with Dylan and the baby. Dylan's mother always worked, and he stayed in day care or with relatives. He would want me to stay home, assuming he could afford to support us with the salary from his computer job. He worked out a way that I could contact other adoptees and I've started to e-mail some people. I've gotten a few interesting responses, too.

One woman who had written a few times is actually a dialysis patient, like my Mom. Because she's adopted, she doesn't know if other people in her biological family have kidney disease or not. Her social worker at the dialysis unit is helping her to do a search. Not only to find out about her family, but also because they might be potential living related kidney donors for Tina.

Another young woman named Kelli has been writing to me also. She says her adoption was an illegal one, and no agency was involved. She has a photograph of her birth mother, which was given to her by her adoptive mother on her 18th birthday. She says she stares at the photograph all the time, but hasn't had the courage to start a search yet.

The letter continued, detailing information about the adoptees that Pamela had contacted. Rachel grew worried that the letter would end without any other reference to her pregnancy. Pamela began to inform Rachel about her relationship with Dylan, and she spoke positively about their interactions. Dylan sounded like a young man who was able to treat Pamela well. He wanted to do the right thing. He felt protective of her and the baby. The subject had resurfaced.

I have some time to weigh the options. To really sit down and talk things out with Dylan. He's very honest with me and I like that. I called Tracy last night and she was very supportive. I'm not isolating myself and I'm not depressed about my situation. Yesterday I was scared about my life taking this direction. Am I really ready to be a mother? But I know I really want to be a mother. Today I'm feeling that I might want to try. If only the timing were better...

I'm sorry if you get this and you feel disappointed that I might not follow through with my college plans right away. I might still be able to take college courses at another school, without matriculating. There are other schools in the area. I could at least get some of the requirements over with. I think my parents would still pay my tuition. Who knows, they might even be happy about the prospect of a new granddaughter or grandson.

I'm feeling more confirmed as I write. A little excited, too. I'll keep you informed. Maybe you could drop me a line? Let me know what you think?

Sincerely,

Pamela Windsor

Rachel quickly jotted down a few lines to Pamela, about being able to support her in whatever decision she makes. She wrote that Pamela seemed to have a good perspective on the situation. She was glad that Pamela was reaching out to people. Rachel reassured Pamela that she was not disappointed in her. She folded the Access Health Center stationery and addressed the envelope to Camp Winnepeg. She put the letter in the bin labeled Outgoing Mail, and reentered her office to prepare for her next client.

Chapter 15

The next letter from Pamela arrived in early August. Rachel noticed the return address right away. Pamela Saunders.

Dear Rachel,

I met Dylan's parents last week, and they were so welcoming that I started to cry. They supported us in our decision to get married, and they witnessed the small ceremony. Dylan has been very loving, and I'm really hopeful that we can work everything out together. His parents offered to help us out financially, and we can stay with them until Dylan settles into his new job.

I'm a little nauseous in the mornings now, and I get tired going up and down stairs. It's so amazing to me that as I'm eating a sandwich or going about my normal routine, my child's lungs are developing! My stomach feels a little hard, and my breasts are definitely bigger. I wrote my parents a long letter about Dylan, the pregnancy, and all my fears that they would be angry and reject me. Surprisingly, both of them called last Sunday, and they're trying to be enthusiastic about the situation. My mother even talked about a baby shower! I've been to a woman's clinic a few times, and everything with the baby is okay. I'm so tired after working with these kids at camp, that I sleep better than I ever have.

On the adoption front, I've become addicted to writing to my e-mail friends. Remember I wrote to you about Tina, the dialysis patient who had started her search? Well, she finally found her birth mother, who was thrilled to hear from her, but she has breast cancer and can't donate a kidney to her daughter. Tina was glad to have found her in time to begin a relationship, though, and will be meeting her extended family as well.

I have some new friends writing to me also. Kelli writes often for encouragement but still hasn't started her search. Daniel is a man in his forties who has a really interesting perspective on adoption. He started his search in the 1970's, when a lot of agencies were not releasing information about birth families. He actually describes how adoption always felt to him like a form of neglect, because of the secrecy. He explains how traumatized he was because so much information was kept from him, and when he finally found his birth mother, the woman didn't even remember giving birth to him! She had repressed the entire experience. Daniel persisted, and now he has a loving relationship with his birth mother, as well as with his brother and extended family. Daniel told me that when he was my age, he had trouble with drugs and alcohol. He thinks he was using them to block out the pain about how he was treated. No one would talk to him about being adopted. There were no pictures of him before he was three years old. His adoptive mother got angry whenever he introduced the subject, and his adoptive father was a strict disciplinarian who used to tell him his parents didn't love him. What a strong spirit he had! The will to find family can be very powerful.

It feels healing to be starting my own family. A mother and child in the same home, growing together, feels like a miracle to me. I think I'll be a good mother. And Dylan is already starting to bring little booties and things back to the camp after returning from his days off. Paul is excited about becoming an uncle. When I'm not feeling scared, I'm very excited. I'll keep in touch. Thanks for your letter.

Sincerely,

Pamela Saunders

Rachel put the letter aside. She was worried about Pamela. When Pamela left for New Hampshire, Rachel felt that she could have done more as her therapist. Now she began to feel some pangs of guilt again. She could have guided Pamela more about relationships. She could have spoken about birth control with Pamela, to ascertain how she would manage to avoid another pregnancy in her future relationships. The topic of sexuality rarely surfaced with Pamela. She seemed embarrassed and naïve about it. Rachel wondered if her own discomfort with the issue contributed to Pamela's silence. When Pamela left Massachusetts, Rachel had felt as if her own arm had been amputated. A large part of her was gone. Pamela had worked her way into Rachel's heart. She seemed so pure and innocent, and Rachel wanted to protect her from life's hurts. Soon, Pamela would have a child of her own to protect and nurture. Rachel had felt her maternal instincts surface in her work with Pamela. Maybe she needed to talk with Glen about being a parent herself. Although her husband wanted children, he was awaiting Rachel's decision, her readiness to become a mother. Perhaps it was time to stop refilling her prescription for birth control pills. Rachel no longer prioritized her work in the same way, especially now that Pamela was gone. She was becoming accustomed to the odd ways in which

Pamela's life seemed to parallel her own. She would talk to Glen. Rachel felt ready. She was resolved to think seriously about motherhood.

* * * * * * * * * * * * * * * * * *

The next letter came in September. It arrived by certified mail, and Rachel had to sign for it. Pamela had written the words *personal and confidential* at the bottom of the envelope.

> *Dear Rachel,*
>
> *We've moved into Dylan's parents' home and life is quite blissful. He loves his job and is actually training to consult with other firms about Y2K compliance. I decided not to attend school and am devoting myself full-time to helping other adoptees. I found another group to attend and have been writing to literally hundreds of people via the Internet. I met my grandmother with Paul the other night, and she told me she's always loved me! And you'd be proud of me, Rachel. I have an on-line bibliography about adoption resources and publications!*
>
> *Yesterday, a young woman contacted me for the first time. She has started a search for her birth mother, and has reached a dead end. She's nineteen years old, and she was born in New York City. She was never given a first name. The name on her birth certificate appears as Baby Abbott. Her mother's name appears as Rachel Abbott.*

Rachel's heart was pounding in her chest. Her head began to ache, and her breathing became difficult. She had to sit down. Her hands began to shake, but she could not put the letter down.

Of course, after reading her e-mail, I immediately searched my knapsack for your business card, to verify the spelling of your name. Two b's, two t's. Abbott-Moss. She lives in Connecticut, and traveled to Long Island, to the address on her birth certificate in Wantagh, New York. She was devastated to discover a FOR SALE sign on the front lawn. No one lived there anymore. She contacted me after she returned home. The realtor was unavailable, and her father's name is listed on the birth certificate as Unknown. She was so saddened by her anticlimactic journey!

I guess it's just wishful thinking, but I was hoping you could help me out with Baby Abbott. Are you from New York? Once in a while, I would notice what I thought was a New York accent when you spoke. You told me both of your parents had died, and I wondered if that's why the house on Long Island was for sale. Could Baby Abbott belong to you? Her date of birth was June 13, 1980.

I'm sorry if you find this letter intrusive, but I know you understand the importance of family to adoptees. I told Baby Abbott (her adoptive family named her Nicole Emma Gordon) that I would try to refer her to someone who could assist her in her search. Rachel, I would feel so honored if she were your daughter and I were the one who brought her home to you.

I wouldn't have written, except that I also downloaded the photograph that Nicole had sent me. Honestly, it scared me half to death! This young woman could be your little sister! She looks just like you. Please don't feel that I'm asking you for any details about your past. I would be glad just to send you her picture, her address and telephone. And to know that ultimately, there would be true reciprocity in our relationship. You've guided me toward my family, I may introduce you to yours.

Sincerely,

Pamela Saunders

She *is* my little sister! I gave birth to my own sister! Rachel crumpled the letter and stuffed it into the pocket of her skirt. Her breathing grew more labored, and she began to perspire. Rachel recognized the signs of a panic attack. Her nausea increased rapidly. Rachel excused herself to the receptionist and ran to the rest room. Dizzy, she could taste her lunch in her throat, and held onto the sink to vomit. Clearly, there was something she could not digest. Her mind raced. Her father had said she had had an abortion! How could a child have been born? Her father was dead. How would she ever know for sure? *The doctor!* What was his name? Rachel couldn't think. She knew one thing for sure, though. The date that had carved itself in her memory forever. Friday, June 13th, 1980. The date that her father drove her into Manhattan. The date that he told the most vicious of lies. The date of her ultimate betrayal. The date that her daughter was born.

* * * * * * * * * * * * * * * * * *

Rachel composed herself and reentered the waiting area. She mumbled to Hilary that she thought she had food poisoning and would be leaving work shortly.

"You look white as a ghost!" Hilary remarked.

"My appointments will have to be canceled, Hilary." Rachel retreated to her office to call Glen.

"Honey, I have to talk to you right away. Something has happened."

Glen heard something very unusual in Rachel's tone. There was almost a desperate quality to her voice.

"I'll be right over. Don't drive. I'll pick you up and we'll return to get your car when you feel up to it."

Rachel thought of her friend Neil. The time he picked her up at the train station after her father abandoned her in the hospital. She felt a similar relief now.

"I'll be outside. I'll wait for you at the entrance to the building."

"Give me about twenty minutes, love. I'll be there as soon as I can."

Glen was true to his word. He drove underneath the building's awning and got out of the car to open the door on the passenger side. Rachel hobbled into his Honda and Glen sped off toward Northampton.

"Do you want to go right home?"

"We don't have to. I just need to talk to you."

Glen drove north on Route 91 to Exit 18, and headed toward Route 9. He stopped the car in front of the entrance to Childs Memorial Park, having no idea how symbolic its name was for Rachel at that moment.

"Do you want to walk?"

"OK." Rachel's dizziness was subsiding.

Glen exited the car and helped Rachel to do the same. She seemed so fragile and weak. He could not imagine what had happened.

"Glen, there are a few things I never told you about my past. Not because I didn't trust you, but because I thought it would haunt me more if I talked about it. My father abused me, but not only physically."

"Sexually also?"

"Yes, but there's more. He raped me, and I became pregnant when I was thirteen."

"That bastard!"

"At first, I wasn't sure I was pregnant. My body felt different, but every once in a while I would menstruate. Maybe I was just spotting, I don't even know. When I started gaining weight, I tried to hide my stomach underneath baggy sweaters. I felt the baby kick. I was connected to it; I wanted to have it. The psychologist at school wanted me to interview at a residence for pregnant teenagers, but I was too young, and needed parental permission. When I told my father, he was furious. He took me into Manhattan and found a doctor to perform a late-stage abortion. At least that's what he told me. I was only thirteen. The doctor hardly spoke to me. He gave me a long exam, and then some drugs that put me to sleep. That's all I remember until I woke up in the hospital. The next day, I moved out of the house. I contacted Aunt Lynn and moved up here."

Glen kept his arm around his wife's shoulders as she spoke. He could feel her body shaking. He fought hard to suppress his rage.

"Today, at work, I got a letter from Pamela, the ex-client who moved to New Hampshire. I've spoken with you about her before. She's adopted, and has been helping other people to search for their birth families. She's using the Internet. A young woman contacted her yesterday who was born on the day of my 'abortion.' The mother's name on the birth certificate is Rachel Abbott." Rachel began to sob. "I'm so ashamed...I gave birth to my own sister...but I wanted her...he told me it was an abortion...how could this be happening?"

Glen held his wife closer. "I don't know, sweetheart. Your father was a real piece of work. First, raping you, then, getting you pregnant, then lying about his decision! I never heard of anything so horrific in all my life."

"Her name is Nicole Gordon. Nicole Emma Gordon. Pamela wants to know if I want to meet her. How could I ever face her? The birth certificate didn't list a father's name, but what if she asks? I would feel so exposed! But if she's my daughter, how could I *not* meet her?"

"Meeting her and telling her about your father are two different things."

"What do you mean?"

"You're not transparent, sweetheart. You wouldn't have to tell her about your father."

"I don't know…"

"You don't have to decide anything now. You've just had a horrible experience. There's a lot to think about. We can just keep talking about it until you figure out exactly what you want to do."

"…Dr. Rust…Dr. Russell! Dr. Russell! I have to call him! He can tell me what happened!"

"It's four o'clock. Do you want to head home to call?"

"Let's go."

Glen's head was aching from trying to incorporate the information he had just heard. Her father was despicable. But this child, if she turns out to be Rachel's, had to be considered separately. Of that Glen was certain. Neither Rachel nor Nicole had done anything wrong.

Rachel called information for New York City and was given a physician's referral hotline number. "Yes, I'm calling to try to locate an obstetrician named Dr. Russell, Dr. Mark Russell."

"An obstetrician? In private practice? Do you know what borough?"

"I don't know. He used to be at a hospital in Manhattan, I don't remember the name."

"The only listing I have for an obstetrician with that name is in Westchester County."

"Do you know how long he has been in practice?"

"We should have that information. Hold on, please…yes, he's been in practice for thirty years."

That fits, Rachel thought.

"Do you want his number?"

Rachel remembered her tenacity in waiting for Dr. Russell to leave his office. She was grateful for her hypervigilance. She had the capacity to remember some details while she repressed others. She remembered staring at the nameplate on Dr. Russell's office door. It felt like she had sat for hours, anxious and waiting. *I remembered his name!*

"Yes, please."

Glen handed Rachel a pen, and she rushed to scribble the telephone number on their nearby phone pad.

"Are you sure you want to do this, Rachel?"

"I'm sure."

A young woman answered her call. "Doctor's office, can I help you?"

"I need to speak with Dr. Mark Russell immediately."

"This is the answering service, dear, do you have an emergency?"

"I do. Can he be paged?"

"I can try. Give me your number. If he's available, he'll call you back in a few minutes."

Rachel gave the receptionist the number and joined Glen on the couch. She held her head in her hands and waited.

The ringing jarred them both. "Hello?"

"This is Dr. Russell, returning a page."

"Dr. Russell, my name is Rachel Abbott. I believe you may have delivered my baby in 1980. I'm sorry to disturb you, but this is a very awkward situation. I was told by my father that I had an abortion. I was very young…"

"…Brendon…Brendon Abbott. Is your father Brendon Abbott?"

"Yes! He's deceased."

"He told you *what?*"

"He told me you performed a late-stage abortion."

"Well, he *wanted* me to perform an abortion. I remember your father well, my dear. He was quite memorable. Actually, a bit difficult to forget. Excuse me, my dear. Very persuasive. Very demanding. I told him that the fetus was viable and I wouldn't do it. When I examined you, I discovered you had a condition called Incompetent Cervix. Have you had other children?"

"No."

"I don't know how you held onto that infant for as long as you did. You must've had some bleeding."

"I did."

"You were more than six months along, as I remember. It was too late for the usual treatment for your condition. The weight of the baby was causing your cervix to dilate. You were almost fully dilated when I examined you. I couldn't imagine a thirteen-year-old bedridden for three months. I decided to induce labor and was able to save the baby. Your daughter was not quite three pounds when she was born. She was hospitalized for several months because of her prematurity. Initially, she couldn't breathe on her own. She had some problems, but she managed to pull through with flying colors."

"She's contacted me...sort of..."

"And you didn't even know she existed. I'm sorry, my dear...I should have spoken with you myself. You were very young. Your father waived parental rights for you. We took very good care of your little girl. One of the nurses on the maternity ward fell in love with her, and decided to adopt her. We didn't involve Social Services. I contacted a lawyer friend of mine, and your daughter was adopted into a very loving home. I have managed to have some contact with her over the years. Nicole is a lovely young woman. If I had known..."

"Thank you, doctor, I appreciate your sharing this information with me now."

"You're quite welcome."

* * * * * * * * * * * * * * * * *

All these years, thought Rachel, spent grieving over an abortion that never happened. It was unbelievable. And now there was a daughter, a lovely young adult daughter, interested in meeting her. How could she refuse? Pamela had taught her about the value of finding family. Pamela had written that she would be honored to bring them together. Rachel pulled the letter out of her skirt pocket to reexamine its contents. She read it aloud to Glen. He was at work in the kitchen, cooking something which smelled delicious. Rachel's bout with nausea had ended. She was feeling a bit more capable of handling the situation. Glen had said that no decision had to be made right away. He was right. She would continue to share her feelings with Glen. His support and clear-headedness had meant a lot to her today.

After dinner, Rachel held Glen's hand. "I appreciate you."

"I know you do, love." He kissed her cheek.

She moved his chin toward her lips and was surprised at the level of arousal she felt. A wave of thankfulness swept over her. Gratitude for his goodness, for Dr. Russell's words, and for Nicole's birth. *I didn't have an abortion. I have a healthy daughter.*

Rachel began to massage Glen's shoulders. They were quite tense, and she guessed that he was still angry at her dead father. This was all new information for him to absorb. She kneaded his muscles expertly. Glen relaxed into her touch, and closed his eyes. She removed his shirt and led him to the bedroom. Glen stretched out on their bed, allowing Rachel to continue to massage his thighs and calves, his lower back and buttocks. The tension was leaving his body. Rachel removed her skirt. Unsuspecting of her intentions, Glen turned over to ask if she wanted a massage as well. She unzipped his khakis and he lifted his torso to assist her in removing his pants. Rachel massaged his chest from a sitting position, and felt his penis pulsating beneath her. She was very aroused. Without additional foreplay, Rachel guided his penis inside her. She leaned forward to allow Glen to undo the buttons of her blouse. It fell to her side. He unclasped her bra and began teasing her nipples. She felt a fire blazing inside her as he glided in and out of her vagina, manipulating her clitoris with the head of his penis. Rachel cleared her mind of the day's events, and made a concerted effort to be present. To allow the pleasure. She breathed into the pleasure and the passion, relaxing her body and allowing Glen to travel deeper into her core. She moved her hips in a circular motion and found the heat emanating from her center nearly unbearable. A tingling sensation that felt vaguely familiar enveloped her clitoral area. Her guttural moans grew louder. She leaned forward again to kiss her husband. He changed his position to stimulate her further. She had never felt so aroused before.

"I'm on fire!" she whispered.

"Let me put it out," came the response.

Glen withdrew from her vagina and maneuvered himself so that his lips and tongue caressed her expertly. Her entire being was focused on his sensual manipulation of her clitoris. He made careful circles around her excitement, and the waves of relief began. Enormous waves produced a fulfillment that Rachel had not known was possible. She cried out his name in ecstasy. He continued until her body relaxed. Afterwards, he held her while she cried.

"Are you okay, love?"

"I'm just fine…and you…are a wonderful lover."

Their lovemaking continued into the night. Rachel tried to avoid analyzing the reasons for her sudden ability to let go. She knew she would eventually understand them. She would enjoy these moments of serenity with her husband. She loved him. She had a daughter to think about. She was fortunate, and she felt blessed.

* * * * * * * * * * * * * * * * * *

A premature child of incest had matured into a healthy young adult daughter in search of her birth mother. It was simply amazing. Rachel's heart ached about the years of deceit. She had some new concerns about her ability to have children. Her discussion with Dr. Russell had led her to believe that treatment was available for her condition, but that any future pregnancies would have to be carefully monitored. She was fortunate he had been able to save her daughter, and that she arrived at the hospital when she did. She decided to reread the sections she had highlighted from her copy of Seat of the Soul. Rachel had been exploring her sense of spirituality since her return from Bryce Canyon. She was certain that although she could not have controlled her past circumstances, she could now make careful choices about her future.

Rachel had thought about bringing her father to justice before his death. She was always too afraid of him to take any action. Like her mother, she was silenced by fear. Her mother had taught her well to keep the family's secrets. She was good at it. She even held confidences for a living. Rachel wondered about her choice of career. What would she have chosen if she hadn't been a trauma survivor?

Back in May, Rachel had actually watched a television news show depicting a story much like her own. A young woman who had been a victim of incest by her father had given birth to her own brother. She eventually found the assistance she needed from the legal system and the police to take her father to court in Wyoming. Perhaps Rachel's father had lied to her in order to destroy the evidence of his crime in her mind. If he could be certain that Rachel would never discover her child, perhaps he considered himself safe from prosecution.

Perhaps, Rachel thought, he is being prosecuted now. And what if I meet Nicole, and she asks me about her father? I could keep silent, or even say that her father had died. I could initially tell her I'm not ready to discuss the circumstances of her birth. I could eventually, over the course of time, tell her the truth. Perhaps this entire experience happened in just this way for a reason. Perhaps Nicole was meant to be here for some purpose.

Rachel had no clue about *her* true purpose. She had thought that her purpose was to help others heal through counseling. She knew she had found meaning in work and in love. She did not understand why she had been given the opportunity to meet Nicole. Or why the opportunity had evolved from her own work with Pamela. She had indirectly discovered her own truth by guiding Pamela to find her birth family. The dynamic seemed more powerful that coincidence. Had the universe conspired to bring them together? Rachel knew now the path she would choose. She would meet her daughter Nicole. And she would keep no more secrets.

Rachel thought of Pamela. Her extraordinary detective work in discovering her birth family. The commitment she had made to other adoptees. Pamela had shown Rachel a perseverance unlike any other. A perseverance guided by hope, and born of a need to belong.

Rachel sat down to draft a letter to Pamela. She thought of her supervisor, Ed Weiser. She thought about the Social Work Code of Ethics. She was certain there was no precedent for a situation like this one. No rules to guide her. For the first time, Rachel set aside her therapist persona and spoke from the heart.

> *Dear Pamela,*
>
> *Thank you for your letter. I have spoken with the doctor who delivered Nicole, and I am certain that she is my daughter. I would appreciate your sending me her address and telephone number so I can contact her as soon as possible.*
>
> *Initially, I felt embarrassed to admit to you that I, too, was part of an adoption triad. I became pregnant when I was thirteen years old. I am very eager to meet Nicole, and to begin a relationship with her. I am very grateful to you, Pamela, for your efforts to bring us together. You have brought new meaning to my concept of family. You have taught me about courage. In witnessing your ability to overcome life's obstacles, I have gained more strength to combat my own.*
>
> *I believed all along that you came into my life for a reason. I have learned a great deal from you. And now, I will know more about Nicole's needs as a result of our work together. A corner of my heart is reserved for you, Pamela, and you have helped to heal my soul.*
>
> *Sincerely,*
Rachel Abbott-Moss

Rachel folded the letter and brought it to the post office. She trusted that meeting her daughter would be wonderful. Her mind was enveloped by a quiet peace. She turned to face the day.